MW00931708

ETERNAL HUNGER

Denise K. Rago

Other Novels by the Author

Blood Tears

Immortal Obsession

RAGO/ETERNAL HUNGER/DEDICATION

To all my loved ones on the Other Side whose presence
continues to guide me;
To my husband Marvin, love of my life.

Acknowledgements

To all the authors whose novels I can't live without and who continue to inspire my own writing; to the readers whose enthusiasm compels me to keep writing; and to Emily Brontë, who described the agony and ecstasy of love like no other writer.

Special thanks to readers Rita Vetere and Rick Kattermann; Eleanore D. Trupkiewicz, editor extraordinaire; and Kelly Jones and Misty Layne of Social Marketing Solution. A heartfelt thank you does not cover it.

Cover image by Andrew Hess, 2017.

Notes

The Château des Singes, or the Château de Folie, looms out of the countryside somewhere in Normandy, France, popular among photographers and history buffs looking to record the decaying remains of a seventeenth-century mansion. It has a scant history, so I have created one, filled with lurid tales of debauchery and blood drinking. I thought it the perfect place for my vampires to rest, hiding from the mortal world while plotting its demise.

~

All quotes used as epigraphs are from *Wuthering Heights*.[1]

---

[1] Quotes throughout are reprinted from Emily Brontë, *The Annotated Wuthering Heights* (Cambridge, Massachusetts: The Belknap Press of Harvard University Press, 2014).

Prologue

Somewhere in France

There isn't much I haven't seen in my long life.

When I fell to earth, it was to escape the wrath of the archangel Michael.

I somehow believed that becoming a vampire would keep me hidden from my enemy, but sometimes I can feel him, lurking and waiting.

Christian was an infant, fresh and new, the union of his mortal mother and me, the first time I held him in my arms.

The second time I held my son, his mother had just died. He was eight years old and lost without her. Though I did not have the capacity to weep, I took pity on the child, caressing him while he slept. The year was 1745. The village: Meudon, France.

I chose to protect him from those of my kind—the Ancient Ones who believed that the child of a vampire and a mortal would rise up to destroy them. I scoured Europe, eradicating those who threatened our order, and yet I was a hypocrite, the one who held the very key to the prophecy: a little blond-haired, brown-eyed boy who grew up to be a stunning man.

He never knew of his gifts, nor would I ever show myself to him. At least, that was what I told myself, until I had the brilliant idea to kill my king and queen, release all the Ancient Ones from the bonds of our coven, and make my son the ruler of all the vampires in France. That was ten years ago.

The last time I held my son, his world had vanished in flames. I had to make some terrible choices.

Parenthood is never easy.

PART ONE

Be with me always—take any form—drive me mad.
Only do not leave me in this abyss, where I cannot find you.

Chapter 1
Amanda

2010—Venice Beach, California

I feel the child move, which rarely happens during the day, or while I sit at the bar inside Michel's, watching my vampire lover mix drinks, talk on his cell phone, and flirt; but as I lie in the darkness of my tiny bedroom, in my even tinier cottage, butted up against the Pacific Ocean, I feel a tugging sensation, my womb moving in rhythm with the waves. Although I do not show, I am six months pregnant with the child of a vampire—not Michel, with whom I share bed and board, but his best friend and my former lover, Christian Du Mauré.

It's complicated. I suppose I'm lucky to have gotten out of New York safely and to be living here in Venice

Beach with Michel. He doesn't express it, but sometimes I wonder if he feels as I do, abandoned and confused and so afraid of the future. So stupid, we were, to think that the past was behind us, neatly filed away—done with—forgotten … but the past is never really "done with" or "gone," is it? The past lingers just beyond our reach, ever present and watchful.

As a child, I read L.P. Hartley's novel *The Go-Between*. To this day, the first line resonates with me: "The past is a foreign country—they do things differently there."

How stupid you are, Amanda Perretti, I tell myself.

I once believed it to be true, but now I know better. The past is a powerful specter that took Christian away from us, burned our town house to the ground, and forced Michel and me to flee New York and settle here, in California, so uprooted and disconnected from all we knew that it begs pause.

Now Michel owns a converted warehouse, aptly named Michel's, and seems to have found a way to carry on by doing what is familiar to him: replicating his life in New York and living among mortals.

My nightly routine finds me sitting on my favorite barstool, watching him bartend and try to blend into the mortal world he loves so well. Michel, though, was never able to blend in anywhere, whether at the court of Louis XIV or in a bar in SoHo. He's too exquisite a being, with long, dark curls, emerald green eyes, high cheekbones, and porcelain-like skin that generally glows but darkens to appear almost human-like when he has taken blood.

He and I have carved out a tenuous existence here in California, a truce of sorts, as we figure out what comes next, and although neither of us talks about the trauma of fleeing New York City with literally the clothes on our backs, losing Christian, or anticipating the birth of my child, that trauma seeps into everything that we do.

Michel may be a two-hundred-and-fifty-year-old vampire, but in this case, age does not bring wisdom. He appears to be as scared and lost as I am, and so we wait and wonder about the fate of the one person we love above all else, the glue that holds us both together, the possible father of my unborn child.

Yeah, it's complicated.

Christian, where are you?

Chapter 2
Christian

2010—Château des Singes

It was the smell that woke me. Dampness, mold, abandonment … long-forgotten places.

I inhaled in jagged breaths, forcing myself to remain calm. I was no longer pinned to a wall but laying prone on a rotted mattress on a rusted bed frame. Chunks of pale blue plaster littered the floor. Sitting up slowly, I felt light-headed.

If I were mortal, I would have vomited.

Where was I?

The lone bed was dwarfed by the high ceiling, a promontory among concrete and debris.

How long had I been here, wherever *here* was?

On the far wall was a broken and faded mirror. Not a bad place to start. I took stock of my appearance in a sliver of what had once been a gilded eighteenth-century looking glass. I was dressed in blue jeans, boots, and a green sweater, none of which were mine, yet all in good taste. My hair was clean, free of dried blood.

Not bad, though I wondered who had taken the time to clean me up and dress me like a modern man.

I was not hungry yet, just confused as I tried to piece together the events leading up to this moment. There had been a heavy curtain of falling snow. Josette calling my name. A handsome face gazing up at me through torchlight, giving the memory a tinge of warmth, despite the darkness.

Ghislain. Yes, that was his name. He was connected in my mind to images of monoliths and angels. How baffling.

Just enough sunlight fell through the French windows, illuminating painted wall panels, and me.

Yes—sunlight.

Imagine me, Christian Du Mauré, a two-hundred-and-fifty-year-old vampire, able to walk in the sunlight. Not bright, summer sunlight, which I could not really remember experiencing, but more muted autumnal rays, which give the illusion of warmth yet cast long shadows.

I had my mortal lover, Amanda Perretti, to thank for such a gift. It was her blood that contained such power and had saved my life.

Amanda.

Would I ever see her again?

I had abandoned her, along with my best friend, Michel, in New York City. What a coward I'd been, for I could do no better than leave them a note. What a disappointment I had turned out to be to the two people I loved the most.

My gaze fell on the faded painted wall panels behind the mirror, on which the sunlight landed. It took me a moment to recognize the image still showing through.

Monkeys.

The Château des Singes—the house of monkeys.

Centuries ago I had come here. Though its location had been a secret, it was rumored to sit in the forests on the Normandy coast. Michel and I had wandered through enough Parisian salons to hear talk of the lurid parties, human sacrifices, and the like that had gone on here.

At the time, I had ignored such talk, chalking it up to nonsense, but I knew now that anything was possible, and so I tried to recall everything that I could remember about this place. Memories of long carriage rides with my maker, Gabrielle, and Michel began to assail me. God, we had been so young, even for vampires.

I studied each wall panel, trying to put together the time line of events, but my mind was still foggy. I checked my pockets on the remote chance that I had my cell phone. They were empty. Across from the bed, decrepit French doors opened out to a hallway. I risked it.

Out in the corridor, the diagonal blue-and-white-tiled floor stretched before me like an ocean. I continued walking down a main hallway, passing through more doors with rooms to my left and right. Some of them were actually furnished, while others held only a chair tipped on its side or a rotting divan.

When we'd come here before, the Château des Singes had been a stunning monument to French sensibilities, but now it had been abandoned for centuries. My guess was that it had been built in the seventeenth century, when houses were more ceremonial and less practical for everyday living. Nonetheless, large groups of mortals had come here during the summer months because, as with Versailles, aristocrats summered outside of the dirty, noisy city of Paris.

I wandered farther down the hallway, dodging concrete piles and jagged glass, until I reached a magnificent white marble landing and a massive staircase with a wrought-iron railing of the most delicate design. The setting sun streamed through the many sets of broken windows that faced the front of the house.

Taking the stairs two at a time, I landed in the foyer. Despite its grandeur, there was something about this house that made my skin crawl. I made my way through the carcass of an age long past, and asked myself how I could ever have forgotten?

Chapter 3
Christian

1786—Château des Singes

The Château des Singes stood in a thick forest on the outskirts of Paris, waiting like a wild animal to pounce as our carriage transported Gabrielle, Michel, and me on a winter's evening. Traveling northwest out of the city, we passed darkened villages set back amongst dense forests. The humans lived in small cottages, weatherworn and hemmed in by large maple and oak trees. Though I had grown to love Paris and rarely ever left the city, my curiosity was piqued by this journey.

My mind wandered while our carriage raced through the French countryside. Gabrielle prattled on about the owners of the château, the Pilou family, who had built the château in the seventeenth century. Not much was known about them, neither where they'd come from nor where they'd gotten their riches, but they mingled freely with vampires, and, as Gabrielle put it, they supplied us with privacy and more mortals than we could ever have imagined.

I glanced across at Michel, knowing what he was thinking. He could not wait to get to the party. I, on the other hand …

Lately, I had been distraught, and even a bit jealous of Josette, my mortal lover, and her husband, for he could give her what I could not: a child. In early December, she had given birth to a daughter, Solange, and now rarely left their apartment in Paris. Not that Josette did not relish being a mother—but now she had another being to take her away from me.

We vampires could father no children. The dreams I had had to let go in exchange for wandering the earth forever had destroyed me in some ways. I was trapped in a body that would never age, despite my changing opinions or desires.

"What is it, my love?" Gabrielle smiled, taking my hand in hers. Her dark dress flowed out around her like black rose petals melting into the darkness, while her breasts glistened milky white like alabaster. She had to sense my distance and lack of interest, for although I found her beautiful, I was so much in love with Josette that I had lost all interest in my maker.

"Just thinking." I smiled back, slipping my hand away under the pretense of brushing my hair from my eyes.

"We have quite a ride ahead of us." She winked, running her hand up my leg.

I dared not look at her.

Eventually, she turned her attention to Michel and slid across the carriage to sit beside him. She pulled him towards her in an embrace, while he tugged at her bustier, breaking the laces. When she bared her fangs, he obeyed and threw his head back in surrender so that she could pierce his neck and latch on. As she was our maker, neither of us could refuse her our blood.

I stared out the window, watching the forest fly by. Behind me, Michel moaned as Gabrielle drank from him, and I could not help turning to watch when she loosened his trousers, laid him back on the seat, and slowly lowered herself onto him.

If I had still loved her, I would have joined them, but I did not love her anymore, and so I closed my eyes and drifted off, while their thunderous orgasms shook the carriage.

It was not a good sign that I was so bored with this life. I loved the power I wielded over most mortals, but there had to be more to life than parties with Gabrielle and illicit sex.

It was nothing I could talk to Michel about, for he lived for parties, sex, and blood, which he craved like nothing else.

I wanted a solitary life, but Michel would never hear of it, and the thought of separating from him was not one I could entertain. We had been best friends since we were children in the early eighteenth century. I dared not sabotage something that meant the world to me.

Michel was pulling up his trousers and Gabrielle putting herself back together when I saw lights in the distance, blinking through the massive oaks. We slowed down and turned right down a dirt road through an open field. Like a monolith, a three-story mansion jutted out of the landscape. Two side wings flanked the main hall with evenly spaced windows and a slate mansard roof. The house had a balanced, stately look.

As I later learned, however, appearances could be deceiving.

Large manicured hedges framed the long gravel driveway. Although beautiful, the Château des Singes was not very welcoming.

We joined the line of carriages creeping up the driveway. A sentry opened each carriage door, bowed, and escorted the occupants up to the house.

When it came to be our turn, Gabrielle was escorted out, and we were ignored, but not before she asked our coachman to return an hour before sunrise, which, in December, gave us hours of darkness to play.

We followed her up to the massive front door, where she presented an envelope to the pallid doorman, who was dressed in fashionable knickers, a frock coat, and a white powdered wig.

"You will never forget this night, I can assure you," Gabrielle promised us.

She was always good on her word.

Once inside, a sweeping white marble staircase with a wrought-iron banister emptied into a massive foyer lit by numerous torchieres. Mortals wandered past me with their clinking wine glasses and all colors of beautiful silk dresses. A middle-aged couple stood on the staircase, surveying the crowds. I assumed they were our hosts, Monsieur and Madame Pilou.

There was nothing petite about Madame Pilou. Even as she stood on the landing above, surrounded by massive ceilings and marble, she was a big woman, with a bovine face overpainted with rouge and lips so red she looked almost clown-like. She clearly was trying to hold onto her youth, though by a thread, I dare say. The man beside her, likely Monsieur Pilou, was tall and lanky, with sharp features and dark, predatory eyes that scanned each female guest. He appeared wolf-like to me.

Indeed, I might have been one of the undead … but the Pilous made me uncomfortable, despite their stately home and seemingly good breeding.

Josette, however, would have loved it all. No doubt Monsieur Pilou would have been captivated by her, too.

I joined the flow of the crowd behind Gabrielle and Michel, following them down a long corridor lined with paintings and numerous torchieres, which emptied into a massive ballroom. I must admit, I always compared the works of other painters to my own. I found the painters of my own time boring, at best.

Suddenly, the crowd stopped moving. I heard music and slipped through the masses until I reached the ballroom.

My breath caught in my throat. The room was beautiful, illuminated by two large chandeliers and a massive fireplace opposite the doorway, with a large mirror over the mantle. One wall was all mirrors, in imitation of Versailles. The candlelight reflected off the silk material of the women's gowns and their glittery jewels. All the mirrors caught and threw the candlelight back onto the guests, so the room had a warm glitter.

A quartet of mortals, hidden next to the fireplace, played beautiful music. The room was bursting with melody and laughter. Vampires were quiet, predatory creatures, and mortals, all words and laughter.

I was never much of a dancer, not like Michel, from whom I had become separated and who had already found a young mortal to dance with. Gabrielle was nowhere to be seen. I scanned faces, looking for her, to no avail. Women in dresses of all colors swirled past me, not a distraction but a kaleidoscope. I finally found my way to a corner just to watch.

Josette would have loved all the gaiety. I suddenly found myself angry with her for not being more careful. For having a child she had not wanted. How irresponsible … but no, it was not really that; it was simply something else to take her away from me, from our love affair.

I would only have danced tonight with her, but she was in Paris, and who knows what would become of us.

I had had enough.

But as I turned to go, I noticed a man standing by the far fireplace, and the door to my memory opened for a moment. He was tall and unusually dressed, more rustically, not in silks, frock coats, and high-heeled shoes. His intense eyes studied me rather than the passing scene.

When my gaze met his I sensed a familiarity between us. I knew him from somewhere—but where? I had only been a vampire for thirty years, and this place was the farthest I had ever travelled … yet I knew him, somehow.

I watched him as the lyrical music filled my senses, along with the smells of sweat, blood, and wine. So many sensory impressions made me dizzy, and I began to become aroused by the heartbeats around me. I had purposefully fed earlier, but suddenly I was ravenous.

I moved into the hallway before I lost control. When a young mortal woman came towards me I grabbed her before she could pass and pulled her against me, and as she smiled up at me I dragged her into a dark alcove. She embraced me, ready for a kiss, but all I wanted was her blood. Plunging my fangs into her warm neck, I closed my eyes and fed, draining her along with all my anger and frustration.

"Let her go before you kill her." A raspy voice filled my head above the music. How was that possible?

Reluctantly, I released the girl. Her eyes had glazed over. I caught her before she fell to the floor.

Shaking his head, the tall figure urged the girl into the ballroom, where she was enveloped by the crowd, and turned his attention back to me. His hair, the color of fire, hung to his shoulders. He was something more than a vampire. His energy confused me, making it difficult to understand what he was or what he was doing here. His dull brown cape smelled of the earth, and his boots were scuffed and old. No one seemed to notice how out of place he seemed, or if they did, they said nothing. Could no one see him except me?

"Have we met?" I asked. All other sounds fell away, and I found myself lost in his dark blue eyes.

Then he took my hand like a child and led me out of the ballroom. His touch was unsettling, almost as if I were humming a tune, but the lyrics eluded me. He was a stranger, yet we connected—there was that familiarity about him— and so I allowed him to take me back into the foyer, up the incredible staircase with the magnificent wrought-iron railing, and down a long hallway painted sky blue with murals of monkeys lining the walls.

There were monkeys everywhere.

I found it difficult to focus.

What was going on?

The hallway was lined with rooms. From behind the closed doors, I could hear the sounds of mortals laughing, entertaining their undead guests while the vampires fed. Other mortals were in the hallway, pinned up against the painted walls, dresses pulled up and vampires drinking freely. Blood flowed from pale, white necks. Mortals and vampires moved as one in the acts of blood drinking and fornication. I was unsure where to look—there was so much happening all at once, and the smell of blood would have paralyzed me had I not just fed. At one point, I stopped, frozen, until the red-haired vampire took my hand again and led me to another doorway. I heard familiar laughter, which made me pause. I knew that laughter.

Pulling away, I pushed into the room, not caring about the intrusion.

Chapter 4
Christian

A roaring fire was the only source of light illuminating the typical eighteenth-century furniture. I focused on the massive bed near the fireplace. At first, I saw only a pale shoulder and one leg. It took only a moment to realize that I knew every inch of that body.

My Josette.

Her beautiful face was half-hidden behind long, dark curls, her dress in a heap on the floor. A massive pale body—was it my host, Monsieur Pilou?—moved over her, kissing her face and neck. She moaned in ecstasy with every thrust.

I watched in silence, transfixed at the horror. What was she doing with him?

Did she not realize that Gabrielle was here and would kill her on sight?

Clearly, she knew Monsieur Pilou from another time and place, but was this rendezvous more important than the risk to her own life?

I backed out of the doorway. I had seen enough. I stumbled, felt myself falling. Then strong hands grabbed me.

The tall vampire pulled me into the hallway. "The witch will never be yours, Christian."

I was speechless. How did he know my name, or that Josette and I had been lovers? "Who are you?" I managed to say, though my voice sounded tinny and far away.

"Your savior. Leave this house and never return—do you hear me? There's nothing for you here."

* * *

Now I stood in the doorway of that very same bedroom, now crumbling with the rest of the château. So much had happened to Josette and me since that night. I had kept my word to the stranger, whom I had learned was my true father, and never returned to the Château des Singes. Michel and Gabrielle had continued to go often, and I supposed that Josette had, too. As much as I loved her, Josette would never truly be mine. I had never spoken to her about that night.

Four years later, the Pilou family had mysteriously disappeared. Michel and I had already been in London some time when I had noticed an article in *The Daily Courant*. Apparently, Monsieur and Madam Pilou had fled their estate one night, never to return—or, at least, that was what the article had surmised. I'd wondered, at the time, if my father had had anything to do with their disappearance. Had he tried to warn me?

But I shook myself back to the present, to the decayed walls around me. I needed to leave this place and find my way home to New York. *Let Ghislain follow me*, I thought, heading back down the hallway towards the elegant staircase and the massive front door, with its broken windows and loose boards. I did not belong here, and the quicker I could leave, the faster I could get home again.

I reached for the massive brass door pull. The next instant, I found myself in a heap on the floor, as if the door had actually pushed me back. I had careened onto the marble floor quite hard. I tried again and again fell sprawling.

There was just enough sunlight for me to make out Ghislain's outline on the edge of the shadows.

"Don't even think of breaking free." His raspy voice chilled me. He emerged from the shadows with his cape flowing behind him. "This house has been bound with charms and spells to keep you in."

This was crazy. I had to reach Michel. He had to be so worried about me. So many questions rushed into my head as I fought to stand up again. Memories of Josette, Amanda, and Michel filled my heart. "What do you want with me? Please give me my cell phone, now," I demanded, surprised at my own nerve. "I need to call Michel."

I thought I heard Ghislain chuckle. "You need not worry about them." He continued, "Nothing exists for you in the New World, Christian. Amanda and Michel have made a life for themselves in California. Michel is taking very good care of her."

"Are they safe?"

I sensed a smile, but his features were so naturally rigid that it was difficult to tell. "No one can know that there is another child coming," he said. "Believe me, vampires have long memories. After what happened to Mathieu, I am taking no risks this time."

"I saw Mathieu," I said, and told him the bizarre tale: how Josette had had me focus on a mirror, and that Mathieu had appeared on the other side, talking to us as though he were still alive. It had terrified me, and yet Ghislain did not seem at all surprised.

Ghislain tipped his head. "Mathieu," he said, "was murdered in the early nineteenth century."

Like barbs dipped in fire, his words pierced my heart, filling my head with images too horrid to imagine. He had said it so calmly that I sensed he was still angry over my son's death.

Ghislain raised his hand as if to ward off more questions. "I will say no more about his death, but you must understand who your enemies are and how they would undermine your ascension to the throne."

His voice moved over me like water, both soothing and hypnotic. He went on and on about my destiny, which made me feel even less sure of seeing Michel or Amanda ever again. Why couldn't I just be left alone? I wanted my solitude, nothing more. Could he not see it?

Ghislain said, "Though I have watched over you since Eléanore held you in her arms and kept you safe, there is a destiny that awaits you. I have made sure of it."

Eléanore? "My mother? What was she like? How did you meet her?"

The shadow of a smile crossed the ancient vampire's face. Then it was gone. He sat down beside me. "Magical, kind, strong-willed. I did not foresee that she would die so young."

"I must confess, I can barely remember her face, but her voice has never left me."

"She was a beautiful woman, and I … The last time I saw you both, she asked me if I wanted to hold you. You were so tiny and warm. She begged that I take you both away, but I could not, and so I left you with her, though I managed to keep you safe for the destiny that I have been saving for you for centuries, Christian."

I studied his auburn hair, which glowed in the last rays of the sun, and his large mouth and hands. I saw myself in his face, but his eyes contained a vastness I could not fathom. He was so intimidating that I could barely make eye contact with him. Indeed, he was one of the Ancient Ones. "And, Mathieu … he was special, too?"

"He was," Ghislain said, "and although it is true that Madame Delacore accepted my proposal of immortality, she knew I was the only one who could truly keep Mathieu safe. She promised him to me in exchange for my blood. She then had to renounce all contact with you."

Josette had been powerful in her own right. She, a psychic with blood that had called to both Michel and me … now had inside her the blood of Ghislain, a being so ancient that he was beyond my comprehension?

"She was a good mother," he went on, "and she loved Mathieu—and yes, despite being vampires, she and I provided for him in all ways. But boys will be boys, and his curiosity became his downfall. Neither Josette nor I could protect him from other vampires, especially one so seductive and manipulative, so full of hatred and so jealous of Madame Delacore that her desire was to destroy the one true tie between the two of you."

I stared at a shard of broken glass at my feet. There had been only one vampire who'd hated Josette and would have stopped at nothing to slaughter her. When I thought back on it now, Michel and I had left her unprotected and vulnerable to our maker, the beautiful and ruthless Gabrielle. I needed only nod to indicate that I knew who Ghislain meant. There was no need for me to say her name.

He saw that I understood. "Gabrielle," he said, "sought her revenge for your leaving her, Christian. You rejected her for a mortal woman and left her, taking Michel with you. No vampires had ever left their maker in such a way."

I listened as he laid out for me the whole of what I had known in part for centuries, and then spoke. "But she came to New York, to Michel and me, seeking asylum. She told me about Mathieu, and the catacombs. I would never have known I had a son if not for her."

Ghislain shrugged. "She is alone now and needs the comfort you were always able to provide for her. Love is a strange and complicated thing, Christian. Perhaps she felt guilty over murdering Mathieu and needed you to find out about him in some way."

Blood tears burned my eyes. "Why did she have to kill him?"

"She seduced him, just as she had seduced you and Michel. She fantasized about removing Josette and living at Vallée d'Arbres with him, but he refused her. She grew furious with him. Once she realized that he would never hurt his mother, Gabrielle killed him."

"I should have realized," I whispered, fighting more tears, "that she would never let us go or forgive us. We did what no vampire had ever dreamed of doing, and we have paid the price ever since."

"Your notoriety spread all over France, making it more unbearable for her." Before I could say it, he shook his head slowly, as if he read my mind. Perhaps he could. "I will take care of her when the time comes."

"Why have you waited so long?" I had to ask.

"In all honesty, it was for the same reason that Madame Delacore still walks this earth: you, my son. You could not bear to live in a world without her, and you always held out hope that she lived. I could not ever bear to let you lose hope, nor could I imagine your pain if that reality ever came to be. As for Gabrielle, she has been rendered impotent and can bring no harm to you now."

"Amanda always sensed that Josette was still alive. I thought she was simply jealous of my past and could not let it go, but she was right."

"Your Amanda is very powerful, Christian, and she must be guarded carefully, for as much as Gabrielle hated Josette, Josette will slaughter Amanda if given the chance."

"Does she have any idea where Amanda is?" I quelled my tears though I could not stop shaking.

"The question you must resolve for yourself and your future is not an easy one. You have a mortal lover who has just given birth to your son. Though full of vampire blood, your lover is still mortal. Then you have the love of your life, waiting to destroy them both. Josette is a powerful vampire, Christian, which gives her distinct advantages."

"And Michel—"

"He loves you, Christian; only you. These women have been dalliances for him, but in his heart, there is only you. Right now, he is watching over Amanda, protecting her, because he knows what she means to you."

"He is a *roué* who could never commit to anyone …" I closed my eyes, trying to visualize Michel keeping house with Amanda and a baby. It was almost laughable.

"Only you, my son. He loves only you."

"I love him," I confessed, quite sorrowfully, "but not in that way."

"You will need someone at your side who is vampire."

"What in the name of God are you suggesting?"

He smiled ever so slightly.

I should have been terrified, but I was not, for I knew he would never, ever harm me. I was his beloved son, vampire and part something else, which I could not even begin to understand. "I have never wanted to rule anyone," I said. "I am a loner. I always have been, even when I was mortal. I loved this country, but I fled, hoping never to return. France has not been my home for centuries." I did not meet his gaze. "I do not belong here."

"You do not have a choice, Christian. You must rule here, in France. New York is a closed chapter now."

"Why do you want *me*? I no more want to rule than I want to eat a mortal dinner! I only wish to be left alone in a world of my creating, not yours."

"Your fate was decided centuries ago when I fell in love with your mother and bedded her, knowing that I was changing the course of history for all vampires."

And his tale began.

Chapter 5
Ghislain

1720—France

It was the year of our Lord 1720. I rode for days in the midst of falling snow and freezing rain. Although I did not feel the cold, my mount suffered terribly, and I knew the horse would die if I did not find shelter soon. My cape was frozen around me. Only one thought sustained me: seeing Eléanore again. I had seen her only once since she'd given birth to Christian. She had let me hold him in my arms and kiss him.

To know that I had created him staggered me.

She had begged me to take her away with me, but I knew it could not be. Now, the memory of them sustained me down every dark road I traveled in the service of King Raven and my queen, Raine.

I was one of the Ancient Ones, which made me a creature of neither the darkness nor of the light. I existed somewhere between the two, having long ago given up my need for blood. I wanted only solitude.

There were seven of us, born in different times, who had come together to form a council to oversee all the vampires of France.

It was not as though we ruled the others. They, in fact, had no idea that we existed, and we preferred it that way. If one of the lesser bloodsuckers ever met with us, it was because their life was over, because they had done something we could not abide.

Over the centuries, a prophecy had taken shape and form, and had become such a real threat to our queen that I felt very much like the Biblical Egyptians in the book of Genesis, killing the firstborn sons of the Jews to prevent a prophecy from coming true.

Raine feared the possibility that a vampire and a mortal would create a male child and that that child would rise up to destroy her—and, I supposed, all of us. I had lived with her paranoia and her edicts for centuries. I had killed any male child born of a mortal and a vampire that had managed to survive. I had never once been seen, for I charmed each new mother in order to take her newborn child from her. I took my role very seriously, even when one of my kind, Dieu Donné, made a confession.

For, you see, despite being vampires of various ages and backgrounds, we were as susceptible to the call of the mortal world as any other vampire. My friend had transgressed—"sinned," as he put it—and he wanted the woman dead. Her name was Elise. She had given birth to a little girl.

I promised to keep his secret safe, and I tried to convince him to forget about them both, as they were no threat to us, but he was so self-righteous and fraught with guilt that he planned to slaughter them. And all I could do was listen. He felt that it was best he do the deed himself, rather than risk Raine finding out about them, for she might have commanded him to bring them back to her.

Raine was a monster. Though beautiful and blind, she would literally have devoured the child bite by bite, and I had promised myself I would kill mortal children as humanely as possible rather than turn any one of them over to her. I had seen what pleasure she took in bleeding out innocent babies. I could still hear their screams as their flesh was slowly torn from their bodies. I hated her for it.

During the winter of 1720, Dieu Donné found Elise Richard and her newborn girl. They lived in a small village near the town of Meudon. Like most villagers, they lived off the land and had little. Elise was young and poor, and barely able to feed herself, let alone a child. Dieu Donné told me he had spared her suffering, luring her into the woods and whispering calming words into her ear. Tell me about your daughter, he'd said, and in short breaths, she'd spoken of the child.

Eléanore Christine.

While Elise was distracted, Dieu Donné had snapped her neck, then laid her limp body in the boughs of a tall pine, where she would never be found.

He had returned to the cabin, but once there, holding the helpless little girl in his arms, he realized that he could not kill her. Instead, he gave her to one of the villagers and *suggested* she raise her. The young mother took Eléanore with no question and promised she would feed her.

Years later—seventeen, to be exact—Dieu Donné asked me to do him one more favor. Could I return to the village where Eléanore Christine Richard lived and finish what had been started, years ago?

Now I knew he had agonized over it all. Although seventeen years was nothing to a vampire, he felt an incredible amount of guilt. I never thought he would confess anything to Raine, but he had become unstable. It happened, sometimes.

Dieu Donné was almost two thousand years old. He had been a druid priest who had been made vampire in AD 40. He was growing more distant from court, spending more and more time away from the catacombs of Paris. I honestly thought he would have killed the girl himself, but no, he could not do it.

He knew, though, that I could, for I had no trouble taking young lives—or so he thought.

I still carried Eléanore's diary, for in it she described our first meeting, on a winter's night in 1737, when I was traveling under the guise of the king's soldiers, and she was a married woman of seventeen, with brown eyes and thick, flowing blonde hair, the color of wheat.

She had married one Phillippe Du Mauré and was childless.

I had come to her with the intention of killing her, but when I looked into her dark eyes, I wanted her as I had never wanted anything in my long and complicated existence. I was confused and terror-stricken at the thought of not following through for Dieu Donné, but it was too late for me. I charmed her household and lay with her over and over, then gave her an amulet that would protect her and, I hoped, give her the child she had always wanted.

Although I had to leave her, I never stopped wondering about her.

I returned to court, afraid to confess my own sins to Dieu Donné, but I never had the chance to test my resolve. Dieu Donné had left us, which infuriated Raine, though she spoke little about it. I alone knew that it had been his guilt that eaten away at him, forcing him either to confess himself to her or to leave us. He had chosen to go.

To this day, I do not know where he went, or whether he is still among us. Though I tried to reach him through our psychic connections, I never could tell if he had ended his long life or had simply shut the world out. He'd been a loner, never truly accepting the modern world, though I would agree that we adapted, perhaps, but never truly adjusted to any time but our own.

He and I could have commiserated in our betrayal of all that we stood for, but creating female offspring did not threaten the prophecy. I told myself that Eléanore could harm no one, despite her parentage. In that, I was correct.

When I returned to her, one year later, she presented me with our child, a son.

She asked me if I wanted to hold him. How could I say no? All she kept whispering was, "Thank you."

I heard myself telling her how much I loved her, but I could neither stay nor take them with me. I would always protect them, but I would only be able to love them from afar.

Like Dieu Donné, I now had a secret. I never once thought about abandoning my place among the Ancient Ones, even though I now had a son, a boy child who could threaten our order and destroy us.

Christian Du Mauré.

Chapter 6
Amanda

2010—Venice Beach, California

I'm growing tired of sitting on a barstool, and my lower back is beginning to throb.

"Why don't you go lie down out back, Amanda?" Michel suggests, pouring two glasses of Merlot for a tall blonde. Her eyes never leave him.

"Out back" refers to the club's office, the place I find myself handling clerical work and taking calls. It gives me something to do at night and keeps me close to Michel.

I nod, slide off the barstool, and drag myself down the narrow hallway. I punch in the security code. Automatically, the desk light illuminates the tiny room. Michel recreated the office from the Grey Wolf, his club in the East Village, right down to the black walls, the ultra-modern office furniture, and the framed poster from his favorite movie, *Casablanca*. The framed maps of Central Park and Paris are missing—they were painful reminders, to both of us, of Christian's touch.

I toss my purse on the immaculate desktop, slip off my ankle boots, and stumble over to the cold grey leather sofa. Eventually the music fades, and I drift off to sleep.

I find myself in a vast room. The late afternoon sunshine is barely visible through the greasy window panes. The walls are pale blue and cracked, the furniture rusted, and the floor covered in debris.

Suddenly, Christian is there, pacing. I call to him, but he can't seem to hear me.

He looks worried, a common state of mind for him.

"Christian, where are you?" I call again.

He turns, and I reach for him, wanting so desperately to hold him, to feel his arms around me and have him feel his child growing inside me.

Then a dark-haired woman dressed in eighteenth-century clothing looms. I know without question that it's Christian's lover, Josette Delacore. I freeze as she lunges at me. Her clawed fingernails rip into my hand. I pull back, and my blood pools on the tile floor.

"Let him go, you fool," she whispers in a thick French accent. "Don't you see that he is lost to you? He is mine, just as you and your bastard will be mine." She laughs and reaches for me again.

I jump up, scanning the room. I'm alone.

The dream seemed so real that I feel sick to my stomach. I run for the bathroom and make it just in time to throw up in the sink what little I ate for dinner.

When I'm finished, I look at the face in the mirror. God, I look so old and tired. I wash my face and rinse my mouth.

I need to find Christian.

The memory of the dream is fresh, so back in the office, I hit the Enter button on our desktop computer. Google comes up. I type "abandoned châteaux, France," and wait.

Fifteen minute later, I'm still scrolling through websites, mostly of photographers who visited abandoned castles and manor houses in France.

Nothing looks familiar to me until I click on one more link. Images fill the screen, and I know.

This is the place.

The Château des Singes sits in the forest outside Paris, abandoned and in really bad shape.

I now have a name, so I Google other websites until I exhaust my search. Not much is known about the house. A link to an article in *The Daily Courant*, a London newspaper from the eighteenth century, names a couple, Henri and

Celine Pilou, who owned it in the late seventeen-hundreds and mysteriously disappeared. After that, there were no other owners, and the house sits abandoned to this day, crumbling into the earth, taking all its secrets with it.

I print out some images and then begin to Google the mysterious Pilous.

Chapter 7
Christian

2010—Château des Singes

I was not sure how long I sat there, trying to absorb what Ghislain was telling me. He had seduced my mother, and I was the product of their union?

It was crazy.

I would go mad if I did not escape him and get back to Paris. I needed to reach Michel and tell him everything. He would never believe that Josette was still alive, or that Captain Andreas, as we'd called Ghislain, was my true father.

It was almost too bizarre to believe … and yet, it was all true. I pushed to my feet and began to pace, around and then out of the foyer.

Apparently Michel and Amanda were now in California—why California, I had no idea—and Josette was there too. How stupid could I have been? I had left them, and now they were so vulnerable, though I had all the faith in the world that Michel and I could figure things out together. We always had.

But there was Josette.

Could the three of us be together again and rule the Parisian vampires from someplace like this house?

You are losing your mind, Christian.

I wandered into what once had been the library. God, the room was magnificent.

Fireplaces with ornate mirrors flanked both ends of the room, and the floor was the same blue-and-white tile as in the hallway, while massive bookshelves lined every wall. Large French doors opened to the outside. It could have been paradise for someone like me who only felt at home among books.

I turned to find Ghislain in the doorway, as if he had hesitated to disturb my reverie. "It *is* paradise, my son," he said, answering my thoughts as if I had spoken out loud. "It can be rebuilt, and you can live here with your mistress and Michel—"

"And Amanda? What of her, and my child?"

"They must never know what has become of you, Christian."

"Why?" My voice echoed off the marble walls.

"Do you really think you could have both her and Josette Delacore? Neither of them would share you with anyone, and without being made vampire, Amanda does not stand a chance. Let her go. Give her the chance to have a somewhat normal life."

"But he is my child. I want—"

"They will both grow old and die, Christian. What then?"

I stared at our reflections in the mirror. If not for Ghislain, I would never have survived all these centuries. The thought of being with Josette had been a short-lived dream of mine centuries ago—and now here she was. In fact, here were we all: powerful vampires changed by forces we could not even begin to understand. Could we three rule together, be lovers together?

Ghislain's blue eyes glowed, lit from within with a sort of fire, a spark, as if by a glimpse of a future I had never even imagined. I had felt so safe in my world of books and music in my Upper East Side town house, sharing in the ownership of the Grey Wolf with Michel and pretending to be happy in the mortal world.

But I had never really been happy. Perhaps Ghislain, more than most, understood that.

Once again in the gorgeous foyer, I tried to remember the room as it had been centuries ago, to remember every shred of the tales that Michel had shared with me of his experiences during the summer months when aristocrats had been entertained here. He had come here more than once with Gabrielle, while I had toiled away, trying to fit into society as a painter in my portrait studio.

How much time and money would it take to restore this house, not only physically but also emotionally? Michel, Josette, and I had parted in the midst of both an actual fire, and an emotional one, on a summer night in 1790. And the damages …

"What is it, Christian?" Ghislain said. "Are you considering my proposition?"

I sighed. "Michel and I left Josette centuries ago, while Paris literally burned around us. She had stopped begging us to turn her. I thought she had satisfied herself with being lover to us both. She wanted us to be … a threesome, in every way, but we would not hear of it. We would have done anything she asked—"

"Except turn her," Ghislain snarled. "Why do you think that might have been, Christian?"

My face burned as with shame. "I never considered it an option, and as for Michel—commitment, I suppose. He was never one for it, and could not imagine spending a lifetime with anyone—"

"Except you, my son. He would never have wanted her to get in the way of the two of you."

"What makes you think it would be any different now?"

After a pause: "Perhaps we should find out."

I waited, but he said nothing more for the longest time.

At last, he sighed. "I did not trust Josette, if I may be so honest with you, Christian, but I desperately wanted to protect your son in the hope that, one day, you two would meet."

"She told me that you had forbidden her to contact us, and that it was to keep us both safe."

He nodded. "That is true. I shielded all of you from harm. Then Mathieu was … I took very good care of your lover, Christian, but I could not protect Mathieu."

Chapter 8
Amanda

2010—Venice Beach, California

"Amanda, what are you doing?"

Michel is standing behind me. Of course, I never heard him come in.

I lean back in the chair. "I had a dream ... no, a nightmare—but I saw Christian and he was in a decrepit room. ... It was huge vast, covered in mold. I saw these walls with something on them, some sort of animal, and I thought maybe such a place existed, so I've been searching the internet."

When Michel and I first moved here, I would dream about Christian all the time and impulsively shared these dreams with him, but I began to feel like a traitor to Michel, who had taken such good care of me, so I tended to pause before launching into one of my "Christian" dreams, though Michel rarely interrupted or tried to stop me. Sometimes I wonder if I'm able to verbalize what he cannot —fear, abandonment, and worry. Maybe he needs the validation of his own complex feelings towards Christian, and my dreams give him the outlet, too.

"And what did you find, my dear?" he asks, kissing the top of my head.

"The Château des Singes."

The energy in the room shifts. He slides onto the desk and turns the computer monitor towards him. "Le Château des Singes?" he purrs in perfect French, scanning the screen.

"What is it, Michel?"

Without answering, he studies the website, with its numerous photographs of the abandoned château.

"He's alive, Michel, and I know he's there. We have to get the hell out of California and rescue him."

"Rescue him. Come on, Amanda," Michel says, still staring at the computer.

"Please, Michel." I click on a Follow link, then open the second tab. The article in *The Daily Courant* fills the screen.

I watch as he reads it, but I can't keep from speaking again. "I'm afraid that the longer we wait, the more danger he's in. Please, Michel. We know where he is. Let's go."

His face softens in the lamp light. "When the time is right, we will go, I promise you."

"When, Michel? Every day that passes puts more distance between us. Suppose he forgets us."

Gently, he wipes my tears. "Oh, Amanda." He pulls me up out of the chair. "He could never forget you. He's watched over you your entire life."

It's true. He has, for I am a descendant of Josette Delacore—yes, *the* Josette Delacore, the woman, the witch who promised to come for me and my bastard child. From her, I inherited my gift of psychometry, my pale skin, dark hair, and green eyes. Though eight generations separate us, I feel her presence constantly.

When Christian promised to watch over all of her mortal descendants, I was the last, and he did watch over me in New York City, saving my life and sparing me as much pain as possible. Yes, he had watched over all of her descendants, from her vicious, spiteful daughter Solange, to Monique Moulin, a California Gold Rush wife, to Rose Deveraux, a minor socialite born in New York City—my great-grandmother.

My mother, Catherine Richard, had broken the mold by marrying my Italian father, Louis Perretti.

My father was long dead, as are my mother and my brother Ryan. I am the last of the line. I had no idea about any of the dynamics, the family hierarchy, my ancestry, until I met Christian and Michel and learned about their love affair with Josette and about Christian's obsession with her.

It's more than an obsession.

Fetish.

Craze.

Mania.

Even as I say it, I realize that there really are no words to describe Christian's feelings for Josette. And as much as I hate her, I long to meet the woman who captivated both Christian and Michel, the woman who now has me on her radar.

I fear that this will not turn out well for me.

Chapter 9
Josette

2010—Venice Beach, California

My journey with Sarah and Mathieu from France to California had been an uneasy one. Though I had been instructed by Ghislain to leave Amanda alone, I could not, for now was my chance to finally eliminate her and her unborn child. Scrying had aided me in locating them in the town of Venice Beach. Then Sarah found us a house with a lot of windows that overlooked the Pacific Ocean. Quite the view, I had to admit, though my thoughts were elsewhere, having never been a beach person myself. The land was arid and brown, so unlike the forests of France.

I felt exposed, and so out of my element here in California. My only consolation was that this would be a quick trip.

I sent my son Mathieu into Michel's to look for Michel with the specific instruction not to say or do anything, to just observe.

Meanwhile, I had entrusted Sarah with finding Amanda, and so Sarah spent her days wandering the streets of Venice Beach, searching. Once she found her, Sarah followed her back to a tiny white cottage, close to the beach. The shades were constantly drawn and there was no furniture on the front porch, and I tried to imagine the interior, modern and quaint.

I made my plan for Amanda clear to both Sarah and Mathieu. Once I was assured that Amanda was home alone, I would slaughter her there and bury what was left of her and her unborn child in that arid, brown yard of theirs.

"You have a lot in common," Sarah said behind me, interrupting my thoughts. "With your similar histories, I would think you would be a bit more sympathetic—"

"Why—because we fucked the same vampires?" I snapped, whirling on her, then drew a long breath. I needed to stay calm.

It was no surprise that Amanda and I had much in common. She was of my blood, a descendant from a long line of women who not only had special "gifts" but also seemed to attract vampires. We even looked alike.

I supposed I should have been more sympathetic, but Christian had fallen in love with *her*. He had no idea how I'd suffered, or about everything I had endured to keep him safe.

I would be damned before I'd waste any sympathy on Amanda.

Did I feel entitled after giving birth to a boy who, by the very grace of one of the Ancient Ones, had survived?

Of course I did.

Ghislain, or Captain Andreas, as he liked to be called, was ancient and powerful. He had not only saved my life, but had also given me the immortality I craved. He had restored Christian's ancestral home after the Du Mauré family died out, and allowed both Mathieu and me to live there in peace.

It had all been because of Mathieu, my beloved child, but I was no fool—Ghislain's love for Christian was the glue that bound him and me together, and Mathieu would have been heir to the throne of the Ancient Ones if he had not been seduced and murdered as a young vampire.

With Ghislain's help, I had brought Mathieu back through the mirror from the other side of death.

Although he was still, and would always be, my precious son, he seemed distracted now, as if he were listening to a voice even I could not hear. Ghislain had given him some of his blood to make the transition from the other side of the veil. Still, Mathieu remained distant—not disobedient, just remote.

But now that he was among the living, despite being a vampire, I held the key to the prophecy, which I had lost when he was murdered. I remembered feeling empty and lost, myself, as a woman with no bargaining power. Power was an aphrodisiac. Early on, I had discovered that it was my beauty that drew vampires to my bed, but it was my blood that kept them coming back.

While only a thirteen-year-old girl, I had held court at my mother's home, reading tarot cards for the guests, drawing many suitors. Other girls might have been afraid, but I was not.

After my father died, my mother, Beatrice Maraine, had set her sights on a wealthy patron in the hopes of securing a husband for herself, but it was I, a mere child, who had beguiled one of the most powerful vampires in all of France, a beautiful specter name Gaétan.

Chapter 10
Josette

1785—Paris

Josette Maraine waited patiently while the heavyset woman shuffled the cards. One did not have to be psychic to know that most women asked about romance. Women always did. Josette glanced at the ornate clock on the mantle, trying to stay focused. It was only mid-May. The Parisian social season had not yet officially begun, and already her mother was parading her about, using her young daughter's talents to secure favor and, more importantly, a husband.

It had been only two years since her father, Gérard Maraine, had unexpectedly passed away, leaving then eleven-year-old Josette and her beautiful young mother, Beatrice, alone. His small fortune had sustained them, but Beatrice was ready to end her self-imposed exile and marry again.

Oh, Papa, how could you leave us?

Josette watched her mother. Beatrice seemed to float through the luxurious parlor, moving from man to man, urging one after another to sit at the card table and let her "gifted" daughter Josette read their future.

Josette sighed. Her mother was beautiful, wealthy, and an excellent hostess, attributes that Josette thought should easily win her mother a husband—so why the parlor tricks?

She took the deck from the woman, spread out the cards facedown and asked the woman to pick ten. The woman's fat fingers hovered over the cards, a worn set that had belonged to Josette's grandmother, Ernestine. Hesitantly, the woman chose each card, while Josette casually scanned the room.

She noticed a young man, a stranger, just as her mother did, and watched as Beatrice made her way towards him. The fabric of Beatrice's dark blue dress rolled like waves around her as she nodded and smiled and curtsied before the stranger. He was of medium height and build, not much taller than her mother. His trousers and frock coat were deep purple, almost black—an odd color, Josette thought—and the fabric appeared to be silk. His sandy brown hair was tied by a dark ribbon. Something about him seemed familiar, but she shook the thought away as she laid each card before her in the pattern she'd learned from her grandmother.

"She has the gift." How many times had she heard her grandmother tell her mother just exactly that? Beatrice would shake her head and wave her hand like she was swatting flies, but Ernestine insisted that her granddaughter learn to read the cards, and so the lessons had begun in secret, usually when her parents were already in bed. During the winter months, there was little to do after their usual three o'clock meal, so after her parents had retired for the evening, Josette and Ernestine would sit at this very same card table, in front of a roaring fire, and Josette would do reading after reading, memorizing the meaning of each card.

"You need to channel all that power," Ernestine would remind Josette. "Feel the energy each card carries within, study the symbols and images, and then make them your own, child."

How she missed her grandmother, with her sharp wit and kind smile.

Slowly, as the woman leaned toward her, Josette turned over each card and studied it. *If this woman is looking for love, I don't see it here. Wheel of Fortune, the Fool, Death ...*

"Madame Pilou." Beatrice, at their side, gestured with a smile to the heavyset woman by way of introduction.

"Madame Pilou," the stranger repeated, and smiled, as well.

Josette could have sworn the woman across from her melted into the fabric of the Louis XVI chair in which she sat.

Beatrice continued, "Madame and Monsieur Pilou have a beautiful château in the forests outside of Paris. It is quite the honor to receive an invitation to one of their parties."

I have never received one. I wonder why.

"Perhaps," the stranger said, "I would be lucky enough to grace your exquisite mansion one of these summer nights." He took Madame Pilou's puffy hand and kissed it.

Madame Pilou blushed.

Josette had to look away. *Revolting.*

Then the stranger turned quickly to Josette.

"And this," Beatrice said, "is my daughter, Josette."

At her name, Josette glanced up from the cards.

The stranger nodded. "Mademoiselle."

At that instant, Josette fell into his dark eyes and a pair of dimples that gave his face a boyish charm. He took her hand and brushed it with cold lips, and a flush of warmth rushed through her body and settled between her legs. The noise of the crowd vanished, leaving, it seemed, only the two of them, gazing at one another in the ensuing silence.

Still, he looked vaguely familiar. Josette searched his face, wondering where they could have met before, but came up with nothing.

"I was just telling Monsieur Richard how talented you are, Josette," Beatrice interjected. "Perhaps you would like to know your future?" she asked him.

Was that—yes, there was desire in her mother's eyes, even longing for this beautiful young stranger.

The young man shook his head. "Perhaps another time. I have disturbed you enough." He turned to go.

Oh, he couldn't leave now … but how could Josette entice him?

Across from them, and on the fringes of their conversation, Madame Pilou smiled weakly.

"Ah, there you are, Celine," someone said.

Josette looked past her mother and the stranger, where a tall, wolf-like man had approached them and continued to speak.

"Pardon my bad manners," he said. "I am Henri Pilou." Oddly, he was staring at Josette.

She felt herself blushing under his gaze.

Josette's mother rose to the occasion. "I am Beatrice Richard. This is Monsieur Richard, and my daughter, Josette Maraine."

"Charmed." Monsieur Pilou took Josette's hand and brushed it with his lips and the tip of his tongue. When he smiled at her, the floor shifted, and as his dark eyes moved over her body, a passion swelled inside her.

"Perhaps you want your future told, as well, Monsieur Pilou." Beatrice took the newcomer's arm.

"Yes, perhaps."

No one moved. Though still flushed from Monsieur Pilou's touch, Josette knew she would have Monsieur Richard—that despite all her mother's flirting, Beatrice would never win the young man for herself.

"Well, then." Beatrice paused. "May I offer you both some champagne?"

Monsieur Richard looked at her mother as if just hearing her for the first time. "Why, of course." They melted back into the crowd.

"I'm sorry," Josette said to Madame Pilou, gathering up the cards and putting them in their embroidered pouch. The mood had been shattered, and the best Josette could hope for was to slip into her boudoir without her mother noticing. Somehow, she thought it would not be too difficult.

Josette stood up, leaving Madame Pilou with her mouth agape, and made her way through the aristocrats that crowded the parlor, playing cards, smoking, and drinking.

She sensed someone behind her while climbing the stairs. She turned then froze.

Monsieur Richard had followed her.

"Monsieur," she whispered, startled yet unafraid. She was about to ask the whereabouts of her mother when he gently took her hand, guiding her into the shadows. Her knees started to shake as he pulled her close to him, brushing a strand of her dark curls away from her face.

"Do you know how beautiful you are?" he said.

"Monsieur …"

"Please, call me Gaétan." He still held her hand.

Josette tried to look away, but could not. "Thank you, monsieur, but you must be confusing me with my mother."

"She is not nearly as beautiful as you, Josette."

Something about his tone of voice, his words, soothed her, caressing her like silk. "I am but a child, monsieur."

He shook his head. "You are now thirteen, and a woman, no?"

Josette had never thought about it, but her mother had probably been thirteen when Josette had been born. Perhaps she did not feel like a woman—more like a lost child—and yet she was not afraid of this beautiful stranger, who held her with his dark eyes. She wanted to reach up and kiss him, to feel his lips against hers, and felt herself blush again. She had never reacted to a man this way. It both aroused and frightened her. "Perhaps I can read your cards sometime, if you would like to know your future."

He bent his head, brushed her lips with his. Was the room spinning? She hung onto him, afraid she would fall. His lips were cold, but she returned his kiss anyway.

"I already know my future," he whispered.

Only then did he slowly let her go and melt into the shadows, leaving her trembling on the stairs, anticipating his touch.

Chapter 11
Josette

1785—Paris

Monsieur Richard did not return, and Josette grew tired of performing at her mother's parties, but by the summer's end, the parties ceased, and life returned to a more stringent schedule. She would have to wait another year to partake of the social scene, and she wondered how she would get through another Parisian winter.

Retiring upstairs to bed one night, leaving her mother asleep by the salon fireplace, Josette closed her door, then the shutters, and began to undress.

A figure materialized from the shadows before she could scream. "Please, mademoiselle, do not be afraid," he whispered, putting a cold hand over her mouth. "I only wish to make a proposition."

It was Monsieur Richard, dressed in black, his tawny hair falling around his shoulders.

Something tightened in her groin.

His eyes darkened, his skin paler in the firelight.

"You have no need to be afraid of me." His deep voice caressed her. He slowly ran a cold finger over her lips. "You are a most beautiful creature, and for someone who has lived as long as I have, you cannot begin to understand how I compliment you when I say that."

Stunned, she could not speak. As the room seemed to slip away, her thoughts remained jumbled and discordant.

"Your mother promised you to me, Josette, and I have come to collect on her good word."

"She never mentioned to me that you expressed an interest in my hand."

"Your hand?" He laughed, releasing her. "If I were the marrying kind, I would gladly take you for my wife,

Josette, but what I propose has a much greater advantage for us both."

He led her over to her bed and sat down, gesturing for her to join him. "You have a gift that I would ... borrow ... and, in exchange, I will dress you in raiment finer than anything you could imagine, give you sparkling jewels, and show you off at parties among the royals of this city. You have my word that your mother would have a secure future, as well."

He ran a hand down the skirt of her gown. "You are more than just a tarot card reader. You actually see. ... You have the second sight, I believe it is called."

Her grandmother had told her the same thing, when she was just a child. She'd had no idea what Grandmother meant, had assumed that everyone heard voices or saw and heard the past just by touching an object. Once she'd confided in her grandmother, her life had changed, and she'd been exposed to a world most knew nothing about.

How Josette missed her grandmother's guidance. Ernestine would have known what to do in this situation. Josette's mother saw security and comfort for only herself, whereas Grandmother could read people, discern their motives.

What would she think of Monsieur Richard? How would she turn this meeting around to gain the upper hand? Josette envisioned herself walking arm in arm with this handsome young man on the Pont Neuf or in the Jardin de Tuileries, basking in the attention of the royal family, dancing at their parties, dressed in silk gowns, adorned with jewels.

She took a breath. "You must tell me, Monsieur Richard, how you propose to *borrow* my gifts."

"Better yet," he purred, "let me show you."

Before she could protest, he had her in his arms and was slowly pulling the pins from her hair. His cold lips caressed her neck, sending shivers of desire through her body. He brushed her hair back, over her shoulder. She closed her eyes, anticipating something, though not sure what he had in mind.

Then she felt the pinprick.

"Monsieur Richard …" Her own words melted and she went limp in his arms.

He is drinking my blood.

But there was no fear, only peace.

When he released her, his sensual lips were stained red.

That is my blood.

Something stirred within her at the sight of her own blood. It aroused her, and yet she tried to fight what seemed so irrational and unbelievable.

"This is your power," he whispered, dabbing the rivulet of blood running down her chest with his finger and licking his fingertip clean.

She fought to understand his words and the look on his face.

"Your blood is your gift," he said. "It is what makes you so … special."

"Special to whom?" she whispered. "I don't understand.

He laughed, and it was then that she saw them.

Fangs.

He is a vampire, one of the undead.

The truth rang through her head, but she was not afraid. *Has he enraptured me somehow?*

He stroked her face. "Please do not be afraid of me."

He kissed her gently, and she tasted her own blood, still on his lips.

Slowly, he began to loosen her bodice. She let it drop. He drew her up and loosened her skirt. The fire warmed her as she stood before him in only her lace petticoat. Why hadn't her mother checked on her by now?

"She will not bother us tonight." Monsieur Richard gazed down at her. "I have sufficiently hypnotized her."

Josette felt his desire for her, and desire was power. "What is it that you propose, Monsieur Richard?"

"Please." He kissed her gently. "Stop the formalities, and call me Gaétan."

"Very well, Gaétan. What is your proposition for borrowing my blood?"

"I want more than your blood, mademoiselle."

She trembled as he ran his hand from her collarbone down to her navel.

"Tonight I take your virginity, but I give you the world, Josette, if you will have me."

The next moment, his fine silks were in a pile on the floor, and his lips covered hers again. She closed her eyes as he kissed her gently, teasing and caressing her with his mouth and his hands. When he knelt between her legs, she felt herself on fire, afraid she would burst into flames.

She glanced past him to their reflection in her floor-length mirror, transfixed when he pierced her inner thigh. Who was that girl in the mirror, trying not to cry out in pain or appear afraid? She swooned with the rush that began building inside her. Gaétan released her leg and pushed his tongue inside her again.

Oh, the sensation was at first painful … and then she relaxed and leaned into him, surrendering to her own growing desire.

When he stood and lifted her in his arms, she knew what was coming.

Laying down beside her on her bed, he pushed her legs open and climbed between them. Though she tried to relax and move with him, she cried out as he tore into her and warmth flowed out between her legs, likely her own blood—her virginity.

When he latched onto her neck and drank from her, she relaxed, and the rhythm lulled her into a trance.

When she screamed out his name, he shuddered inside her.

* * *

The first time he took her to the Château des Singes, the grandeur of the estate was exceeded only by that of the food and drink, but when he gave her as a "gift" to Henri Pilou, she balked, at least at first. Pilou, however, was not only generous with his body but also with his wealth. Soon Josette found herself the lover of not one, but two extremely powerful men.

If Celine Pilou protested, she kept it to herself, for her husband was not only rich, but also cruel, and so she resolved to leave him to entertain himself with the young girl.

Meanwhile, Josette had taken to allowing more than one vampire to drain her to the point of unconsciousness, a small price to pay for security, wealth, and adoration.

Chapter 12
Amanda

2010—Venice Beach, California

"Enough, Amanda. Let's go home." Michel reaches across me to turn off the desktop computer.

"This is the château, isn't it?" I point at the screen. Still he won't meet my gaze, which means he doesn't want to lie to my face. "What is it about this place, Michel?"

"It's late," he says. "Come on." He leads me to the door. We exit the club and turn right, towards home.

The air is cooler; the ocean, an inky expanse. It's truly beautiful. But Michel is still not making eye contact with me. Passersby move around the stunning vampire, giving him plenty of room.

My phone buzzes with a text message. "Just heading down to Michel's," it says.

"Oh, shit," I say, "it's Sarah. She's coming down now." I stop to text her back: "Really tired, heading home. Can we meet up tomorrow?"

Seconds later, she replies with a thumbs-up emoji. Phew.

Sarah Walker is new to California, just like us, and like me, she's obsessed with eighteenth-century France. In fact, she knows so much about the French Revolution, it's like she lived through it herself. Apparently, she's working on a historical novel about Louis XVI. She has a rich aunt who rented a house for her near the Getty Museum.

If I felt free to talk about Michel with her, I could tell her about him—my walking source of history—but I'm afraid she'll think I'm crazy.

Besides, the fewer the people who know about us, the safer we'll be. Call me mistrustful or paranoid, but after what Michel and I experienced in New York, the less I say to anyone, the more in control of our lives I feel, and lately I have needed a sense of control.

Sarah sometimes comes to the club. I've wondered what she thinks about the clientele, but she never says a word, and I don't ask.

I've even shied away from telling her any more than that the father of my child and I are no longer together.

Many nights, though, Sarah and I hang out at our cottage. She likes white wine, and I have my mineral water. Sometimes we wander around Venice Beach, dine out, and shop. She begged to go along when I began shopping for baby clothes, though I had no idea of the sex of my baby, and we casually tossed around names.

Dare I tell her that I have not once been to a doctor?

Crazy, I know, and risky, but a doctor would mean ultrasounds, blood work, and tests, and I can't afford to have anyone poking around my body. I could just imagine the scene: *"Yes, Dr. Jones, I'm a single woman. No, I do not know who the father of my child is. Oh, and by the way, did I mention that I slept with not one but two vampires before I got pregnant?"*

None of that would be well received. Instead, I read books, eat well, and try not to think about who will deliver my baby.

I've tossed around a list of names for a while now, but the only two that resonate with me are Catherine if I have a girl and Julien if I have a boy.

* * *

Once Michel and I get home, I immediately lock the bathroom door, strip off my clothing, and take a long, hot shower.

A million impulses fill my head.

Dare I book a flight to Paris?

As I wash my hair, I calculate how far I could get if I booked a morning flight. I would arrive in Paris ten hours later and have a true head start, if Michel did not prevent me.

My driver's license is still valid. My passport was one of the things I had with me before our house fire, and still have. I have cash and a credit card. I would only carry my toiletry bag.

A possible hitch: pregnant women are banned from airline travel after a certain number of weeks into their pregnancy. I'll need to make sure I'm on a plane before that deadline. Otherwise, God knows how long it will take me and my child to get to Paris.

By the time I'm in bed, I'm already having second thoughts. I have no way to defend myself in Paris, no vampire at my side to protect me in case we're attacked. And what happens after my baby is born?

As I drift off to sleep, I decide to wait for a sign. Perhaps if I research the Château des Singes some more, and made some concrete plans, I can convince Michel that we need to leave sooner than later.

My mind races.

Who could be holding him there?

"Why won't you tell me about the Château des Singes? Who has the power to hold Christian prisoner there?" I whispered to the darkness, as though it were Michel himself.

The bedroom door opens and closes quietly. Michel. Dare I ask him again?

I feel him slide in beside me, his cold arms wrapping around me.

I'm beyond the point in my pregnancy of making love, but if he tried, would I stop him?

There are times when we can talk, and at other times, no words can express the emotions that well up inside me.

He moves towards me.

There won't be any more words tonight.

Chapter 13
Ghislain

2010—Château des Singes

After all these centuries, Christian and I were together, but I had always known that my son would be hard to convince. He was unlike any vampire I had ever encountered, a true introvert and a loner, which I attributed to his lineage. If I offered to renovate this castle and leave him alone in it, would I face less resistance from him?

I knew he no longer loved Josette herself. He loved only the memory of her. Otherwise, he would have turned her centuries ago rather than leave her to die imprisoned and alone. Michel had no interest in her, either, and Josette? She hated them both.

I left Christian alone to dwell on all that we had discussed. There was no place like the forest that surrounded the ruinous château to restore my sense of calm and to help me ponder what must come next.

I needed to win Christian over to my side … but would he ever grasp the true nature of his destiny? Could he not see how important it was for him to assume the throne and command the vampires, who deserved someone strong and just, with an air of detachment, which he had, and which would serve him well?

Though he would never have admitted it, Christian saw himself as neither mortal nor vampire. He abhorred taking blood but lived, nonetheless, among mortals, for it was their cultural output, their art, music, museums, and literature, which he loved.

He naturally gravitated towards the best of what the human race had to offer but wanted none of the complications of the all-too-human machinations of politics or war.

Perhaps he could not see it, but he had a heart full of love and longing, regret, guilt, and despair, just like any human being. I believed that that alone had saved him from becoming a monster, into which the vampire race tends to morph, despite the romantic depictions of them in literature and film.

Christian had done the unthinkable in leaving his maker, threatening the very order of his kind. He was destined for great things, whether he knew it or not.

And I was the one to lead him.

Josette had chosen him for his heart and sense of loyalty when she had needed a vampire to watch over her daughter. Though she had lied in telling him that he was the girl's father, she had known that his love for her would compel him to do whatever she asked. He had always been so responsible and loyal, traits he'd still not lost, even when he'd succumbed to Gabrielle and become one of her children.

He'd held onto his youth and his mortal life through his best friend Michel Baptiste, who had also become a child of the night and who'd believed, in vain, that Gabrielle would protect them.

Christian had known how untrue it was, for how many times in the mortal world had a father or mother abandoned or slaughtered their own offspring? Why should the undead be any different?

A realist, was my son.

He'd trusted no one but Michel. Now, I had to make him trust me, had to help him see that I was his only salvation and that it was his destiny to rule the undead here in France. There was no one else who could bind together such a desperate group of narcissistic monsters and give them a purpose.

It was his fate.

The changing of the seasons floated on the air. Winter would soon wrap his arms around us all.

And what a place this château was: isolated, abandoned; large enough to hold several vampires without them feeling put upon, for most vampires craved solitude.

I swept through the tall grass until I stood alone, looking back at the elegantly decaying mansion I planned on remodeling and masking to all the humans who came by with their cameras. It would appear as it always had to the tourists, but for Christian and his brood, it would be a masterpiece of architecture, fine furnishings, and libraries; yes, libraries full of books for my beloved son.

This was, however, a world unfamiliar to me, and to manifest this vision of mine, there was only one person who could help me. Closing my eyes, I raised a shield of white light around myself and called out to the one whose friendship with me spanned a thousand years.

Victor.

I whispered his name and reached out, into the darkness, with my mind's eye, imagining him at his typical game of feeding on and fucking mortals in the catacombs beneath Paris. It had been his home for some time, as he loved to mingle with the crazy mortals who inhabited that dark world.

Why would anyone want to surround themselves with the bones of the dead, hiding below the earth?

I took another breath and found myself in the chalky passageways as if transported there, searching for him amidst walls of bones, where skulls stared back at me through the dark holes of their eye sockets. They made my skin crawl, but I kept searching, calling to Victor, telling him to come to me, that it was urgent that we speak. I walked until I felt energy moving through me like a ray of light, warmth and a humming, and I knew he had heard me.

He would join me soon.

I took another deep breath, which seemed to cleanse my mind of the darkness of that place. I much preferred being out here, outside the château, under the open sky full of stars. How I loved forests and feeling the wind caress me. This was the world I preferred, though I knew Victor did not appreciate its beauty. He preferred man-made things, while I needed only nature to soothe me.

I had miscalculated by sending Sarah, Josette, and Mathieu to the New World. At the time I had thought that it was brilliant, only to discover later that they had disobeyed me and were now living close to Amanda and Michel in California.

I knew Josette was angry with Christian, but she would never take her anger out on either him or Michel, and she certainly could not harm me. She would, however, slaughter Amanda and her son, for Josette could never accept another woman having Christian's child, or, more importantly, his loving another woman.

I still fought to understand the bond between Christian and Josette. So much time had passed, they had traveled such different roads ... and yet, here she was, still trying to win him, and he still pined away for the woman she had been centuries ago, and not the vampire she had become. He would never see it, and so he was stuck, just as he always had been.

And here I was, grappling with Josette's destiny. I had once believed that I could never harm her, for to do so would be to kill my own son, but now I was not so sure.

Ghislain ... I am coming ...

I closed my eyes again. Victor, leaving the catacombs. I wrapped my cloak around me and walked farther afield. I did not want Christian to see either of us, and so I moved into the copse of trees that surrounded the house.

Chapter 14
Ghislain

Undoubtedly, I was taking a risk by bringing Victor into yet another one of my dramas, but I had no choice. I had always trusted him and relied on his helping me in whatever way possible. He had kept my secret all this time, and if he'd fathered any mortal male children, he had never told me, despite our relationship and the blood that bound us together. Through my blood, he knew my true identity, and if he was afraid of me, he'd never let on.

I had been hiding amongst vampires for centuries. Victor was the only one who knew I was a fallen angel, hiding from the wrath of the archangel Michael, the master do-gooder of the high heavens.

It sounded absolutely crazy, I knew, but it was the truth.

Perhaps Victor was grateful to be alive after fighting against the Roman legions and almost dying in a battle north of Hadrian's Wall. There had been something about him, his brute strength and confidence, that I had liked and so I had spared his life and offered him sanctuary in the Roman army. When his wounds had festered and fever almost took him, I had given him a choice. He never looked back.

We had seen much together. Though we did not talk much about the past, it bound us together still. My blood flowed through his veins and had given him powers he did not even understand or choose to evoke. I could not, for the life of me, understand why, but in that regard, he was much like Christian. He wanted only to live his eternal life.

But that was where the similarity ended.

I found the swaying treetops hypnotic in their beauty. The wind danced around me. A gust blew past and revealed Victor.

He was dressed in various shades of black with a lace-cuffed shirt, reminding me a bit of Michel Baptiste. They, too, were similar in many ways, loving mortal women and parties like no two other vampires I had ever known. Like moths to flames, they hovered around the mortal world, seduced by its trappings and foibles. Perhaps I needed to bring them together.

Hmm …

"Forever the tree-hugger." Victor laughed, pulling me close. I caught the faint scents of earth and candle wax and blood.

"How's life amongst the dead and dying?" I growled, though I was truly happy to see him.

"It's wild, I tell you." Glancing behind him, as if noticing for the first time where he was, he studied the château for a moment. "This place gives me the creeps."

"The woods or the house?"

"Both, actually, but that decaying monstrosity back there takes the cake."

"It's the Château des Singes, and it has quite the sordid history." I explained as much as I knew of the family that had owned the house, the lurid parties and human sacrifices, while Victor gazed up at the collapsing stone and broken windows. Normally, I hated the dwellings of mortals, but this house was something special.

"Orgies, huh?" Victor said. "Looks like its seen better days."

"Oh, it has, my friend. In its heyday, you would have begged to have been invited to one of the parties here, hosted by two very deviant mortals. More sex and blood than you could imagine."

"No kidding." Victor continued to stare up at the château. "I'm all ears."

"In time, Victor."

"Who's the vampire pressed up against the window?"

I wrapped an arm around Victor. "It's a very long story."

I talked, and Victor listened intently. He was good in that way, not interrupting, nodding at appropriate times. We walked for most of the night.

On our way back towards the château, I explained my proposal about my son's future to rule from the massive château before us, complete with a court of vampires surrounding him.

Victor raised an eyebrow. "Didn't you just destroy our king and queen?"

I nodded, knowing where the conversation was headed. "Yes, I know, Victor. I abhor the very social order that I am now proposing to you, but I want him safe among his own kind here in France."

"There's really never safety among vampires. There are degrees of trust, and bonds like you and I have, but vampires are never safe with one another, just as mortals are not safe around us."

"Christian and Michel have been together for centuries now."

"Yes, but you told me they were friends as children. Their shared youth permeates all things between them."

"I agree, but there is more." I tried to smile, something I rarely did. The expression had always seemed so unnatural to me, so fake and disingenuous. I knew I was taking a risk, but I had no other choice. It had to be Victor. "Amanda Perretti needs to be brought here, to France. In fact, I want you to bring them all here."

"Them?"

"She is with child."

"A baby? Jesus Christ, Ghislain." Victor ran a hand through his thick hair. "Why don't you just kill her and be done with it? Why complicate matters? There's already so much unrest after the deaths of Raven and Raine." He looked out into the darkness as if remembering something horrible.

"You know how vampires are. Killing freely, knowing there is no consequence. Why complicate matters by adding more fuel to an already chaotic fire?"

"There is still more." I then had to explain who Josette Delacore was, her relationship to both Christian and Michel, and why I had to get Amanda away from her.

"So, you want me to travel to wherever they are, kidnap a pregnant mortal girl, and bring her here?" He twirled around with open arms.

"Venice Beach, California, to be exact."

"California? Oh, Christ, I've never been to the New World."

"You'll be fine. There's a wonderful club called Michel's, right on the water, run by a vampire of the same name. He is presently living with Amanda."

"This just keeps getting better."

"Victor." I put my arm around him. "You are the most trustworthy, innovative vampire I know. You are also incredibly handsome and charming. You can get the two of them here somehow."

He turned, and I thought I saw a look of horror cross his features.

"Yes," I said, "you must bring Michel with them."

"The mortals I can handle, but another vampire?"

"I will give you a letter to take to them. Michel is loyal only to Christian. I will appeal to his love for his best friend. Now, there must be some place aboveground where you can hide them. You cannot bring them into the catacombs."

I could almost see his mind working. He loved a challenge, especially involving a beautiful girl. He said, "I think I have just the place. Towards the end of the revolution, when Marie and Louis were carted away from Versailles, there was much looting. I took it upon myself to hypnotize a small handful of mortals, and I ransacked the palace."

I supposed my expression in the pre-dawn light caught him off-guard, too.

He continued, "Those lunatics would have destroyed priceless works of art and antiques and lost a part of their history that could never, ever have been replaced. Once they came to their senses, it would have been too late, so I had to act quickly.

"I moved much via horse-drawn carts under the cloak of darkness, across the French countryside to a small country house in Rouen, far enough away to be unmolested and small enough not to draw attention. Once the stupid mortals had done my bidding, I partied on them all night."

"You ate the witnesses?"

"Absolutely! I tell you, it was a brilliant plan. La Maison des Rêves, I named it. It is beautiful."

I shook my head. "And today, Victor, what is left of this house of dreams?"

"It is as beautiful as the night I left in 1795. It's a stone manor, nothing to look at from the outside, but I have made sure no one will ever enter it, and it's been very well preserved."

"I never knew you were so cultured, or so invested in the history of this godforsaken country."

"Versailles grew on me," Victor said. "Just because a bunch of morons could no longer live with their monarchs … Don't get me wrong, Louis XVI wasn't very swift, but the court was such a magical place, and I kind of had a crush on Marie. I could not bear to watch it be destroyed, so I took furniture, paintings, dishes—you name it." He hugged me then disappeared into the dense forest.

I relaxed. A plan was taking shape. Victor would do as I had asked and return when he was satisfied that we could move ahead. Meanwhile, I needed to give Christian time to digest all of which we had spoken and to feel safe and at home here. I hoped that, in time, he would embrace his destiny.

What other choice did he have?

Chapter 15
Michel

2010—Venice Beach, California

I watched Amanda weave her way through the crowd, coming to join me at the bar.

I had succeeded in deflecting her questions about the Château des Singes for the time being.

Two weeks had passed. I was biding my time, waiting for her to divulge her plan for us to leave Venice Beach and return to Paris. She had to be hatching one.

I had not been back to Paris since Christian and I had fled the city in the summer of 1790. When I allowed myself to remember the early years, when Christian and I had been young vampires, I marveled that we had survived. We had been only boys in the year 1757, twenty years old. Louis XV had been king, and the Bourbons, still in the height of their power. We had lived in the village of Meudon, not far from Versailles, best friends from the time we could walk. Even in our looks, though, we were opposites. He'd loved books, music, art, and solitude—he'd been a great painter—and I had loved women and drink.

I had been young and stupid. Christian … he'd been loyal to the end, and so he'd followed me into darkness in the year of our Lord 1757. What had we known of consequences? He'd simply feared losing me to the seductive Gabrielle, and to the promises she'd made to him.

Neither of us could have comprehended the repercussions of our choices. All we had known was the beautiful and sensual Gabrielle, our lover and, finally, our maker. She was our guide, leading us on a journey of lust and blood as we'd woven our way into the fabric of French upper-class society.

Gabrielle had ruled over the Parisian vampires with her second-in-command, a vampire named Gaétan. What they had not been able to control, they had destroyed. All had submitted to their demands of loyalty and subservience, or died. We'd known there were no negotiations, but I'd simply ignored them, and Christian had never been good at subordination. Further, he had hated politics and wars.

We'd been young and naïve, and had had no idea what we had committed to, and after a time, we'd had to get away from them all.

There was no other choice, for we eventually would have died.

So we'd fled Paris for London, then New York, and then the American West. We'd never remained too long in one place until we'd gotten to New York City in 1901. I remembered us roaming through what would become Central Park, thinking that we had finally come home.

* * *

"You look like you have seen a ghost," I yelled to Amanda over the noise of the crowd. I preferred that she not come to the club, but at times she was so lonely that I could not say no.

She was dressed entirely in black, with small diamond stud earrings. Heads had turned as she'd passed through the crowd, but she seemed not to notice. I knew her heart had been given to Christian and that no one could sway her in her devotion to him. I had thought that he'd loved her, too, but nothing—not even Amanda—could have kept him from Josette.

She leaned close, touching my arm. Her warmth, and the sound of her beating heart, soothed me. "I saw him again, Michel."

"Tonight?" I scanned the room but did not feel Christian's presence. Since we'd had the same maker, I'd have known if he were near. I had not felt his presence in months.

"Yes, just a minute ago. I saw him near those tables in the back."

"Let me take a look." I sighed, hoping to ease her mind. This was not the first time she'd thought she'd seen him at the club. She'd said he had shorter hair and looked younger, but she knew it was him. Since he and I had been made vampire at the age of twenty, I did not know how she could have recognized a younger version of Christian, but I took her at her word. There was no other vampire who looked like him.

I threaded my way through the dancers—or, rather, they parted for me out of habit. Being the owner of the place had some perks. If I didn't find anything, Amanda would ask me if I thought she was losing her mind, and I would say no, and we would do this same dance all over again.

I stopped in the shadows and scanned the catwalk. Multicolored red and blue lights pulsated to the music, playing off the walls of the dance floor, leaving trails on the ceiling. The rooms upstairs, as they had been in the Grey Wolf, were set aside for private parties so mortals and vampires could carouse together alone.

I was at the top of the stairs, about to descend, when something made me glance up. A lone figure crept along the catwalk. His alabaster face was lit red and blue from the strobe lights, and for a moment the resemblance to Christian was so uncanny that I thought it really was Christian.

But this vampire looked younger, and his hair fell only to his shoulders, though it was thick and blond, just like Christian's. How could there be another vampire who looked so much like Christian, who'd been so strikingly unique?

The figure searched the crowd below and seemed to zero in on Amanda at the bar. Though she could not see him from where she stood, he must have had a clear view of her. She was playing with her phone, something she did when she was nervous. She was probably wondering what had happened to me. Had the figure settled on her because she was beautiful and alone at the bar, or was he targeting her?

I didn't remember moving but found myself ascending the metal staircase. Time to find out what the stranger wanted.

To be honest, I wanted to get closer, to see the exquisite creature for myself, but I feared scaring him away.

As I reached the landing, a couple emerged from one of the private rooms, the mortal girl wrapped around the vampire in a hypnotic daze, blood dripping from her neck. The figure turned toward them, and I stepped behind the open door, though I knew he would sense more than one vampire present. The male vampire of the couple was one of our regulars, sated with the blood of his companion, and she had the trance-like look that mortals acquire after having given themselves to us. I had seen it thousands of times.

I flashed back to the night when I'd taken Amanda's blood, in New York. It had been an almost ineffable experience, and one I had tried to avoid again at all costs. I did not want the desire for her blood to become confused with my duty to her. I told myself she belonged to Christian, that we were connected to one another by our love for him, just as it had been with Josette Delacore.

And that taking her blood had been her suggestion and an act of desperation at the time.

As the couple passed, I stepped from behind the door and came face to face with the vampire. It was obvious now why Amanda thought she was losing her mind.

He barely smiled at me, a typical Christian trait. "You must be Michel." His voice filled my head. The blaring music and the din of the voices downstairs fell away. Silence engulfed the two of us.

I shook my head. Amanda had been right. The vampire was the mirror image of my best friend. I was trying to formulate a question when he handed me something. I took it automatically, and in a moment, he was gone.

I dared not waste my time trying to catch him. I ducked into the recently vacated private room to regroup.

The private room was circular with wall-to-wall mirrors. A burgundy leather couch dominated the center. The idea had been mine. Whatever you were inclined to do in private, you could do and watch yourself from all angles. I caught sight of my reflection in the mirror, paler than usual. I was shaking. I sat down and lifted whatever he had given me.

It was a watch. Diamonds caught the light, the rays bouncing off the mirrors on the walls. I turned it over and over. Made of fragile silver, all the pieces remained in place. The timepiece was still running. Before I turned it over, I knew what I would find, for I had given it to Josette for her sixteen birthday, in August of 1788.

The engraving was barely worn. *Il n'ya jamais assez de temps.*

There will never be enough time.

I'd signed the message with my first initial.

It had been true, once. There had never been enough time for the two of us. Josette had been a married woman and had had other lovers, one of them, my best friend Christian. I'd thought that this gift—the watch, its silver chatelaine adorned with objects that had held meaning for her—could encapsulate and quantify my love for her.

I'd chosen silver and diamonds, for that was how I'd seen Josette Delacore: the softness of silver was like her heart, but the shimmering diamonds represented her spirit, her élan and grace. Diamonds were the hardest substance known to man, and I supposed she was that, too.

The chatelaine was heart-shaped, with the timepiece the central focus. Balancing the timepiece on each side were a key to her diary, a tiny sheathed blade for drawing blood, a velvet pouch for her writings, a small vile for potions, and a pendulum for making contact with the dead. A small mirror, the last item, also dangled from the chatelaine, with a silver cover and the initials JD engraved thereon, for her name. The center of the heart had a secret compartment. It had all been so clandestine, like our love affair.

And here it was in my hands.

Where had this vampire—the one who looked just like Christian—gotten such an object? What was he trying to tell me by giving it back to me? That he knew about Josette and me? Who cared? It had been centuries ago.

Or was he simply delivering a message?

Now I sounded like Amanda, all nonsense about Josette still being alive. It wasn't possible.

Unless she hadn't died after I'd left her in the Conciergerie in Paris, in 1794.

We'd made love one last time. She'd begged me to turn her, but I could not. Was I a rake for having left my lover to die alone?

The chatelaine was still flawless, the smoky quartz and diamonds glistening. I carefully placed it in the inside pocket of my jacket and tried to pull myself together. I had to get back to Amanda. With her psychic abilities, she could read it in a second if I let her touch it, but did I want her to know any more about Josette right now?

Back down the catwalk, I paused, scouring the dance floor for the mysterious vampire. He was there somewhere, waiting and watching. Did he know who Amanda was? Clearly she had seen him here before, but had he only been on a mission to give me the watch, with no knowledge of Amanda and her precious blood?

If he was watching me, he would see us talking at the bar, and that might not be a good thing. I could not put her in danger. Suppose he followed her home? Yes, her friend Sarah stayed with Julien when Amanda went out, but they would be no match against a vampire.

I dialed Amanda's phone from the catwalk and watched her answer it. "I don't see anything, Amanda. Why don't you go home and hang out with Sarah?"

"Where are you, Michel?" She looked around, but I blended into the shadows above her, and I knew she could not see me.

I felt stupid, but if the strange vampire was here, I did not want him to connect us. "I am a bit … indisposed at the moment—"

"Damn you." She hung up on me, slipped her iPhone back in her purse and pushed her way towards the door, still scanning the room.

I waited in the darkness until she left, my mind racing, afraid for the first time since our town house in New York had gone up in flames. Who was watching us, and what did they want from Amanda? Surely this was all about her and not me, but we clearly were no longer safe here, regardless. I had been so certain we would remain hidden here in California, but I'd been wrong. The pounding in my chest made me pause until I realized that it was the timepiece ticking in my pocket.

I took a deep breath, had turned to descend, when, out of the shadows, they materialized.

Two vampires; the one who could have doubled as Christian, and a female. Sounds and smells melted away around me as a collage of memories collided inside of me. I grabbed the banister, staring at the female vampire's porcelain face, remembering the last time we had been together.

She'd been slowly dying. A political prisoner in the Conciergerie in the summer of 1794. Selfishly, I'd needed to see her one more time, to sink myself into her warm flesh and take her again, just as she had taken over my heart and soul. She'd been so perfect, so poised and beautiful. The modern world would have swallowed her up, and her uniqueness would have been lost, like tendrils of fog dissipating in the morning sun.

And now she was here. Josette Delacore herself.

A vampire.

I stared into her hypnotic green eyes. They seemed icier than I remembered. Don't get me wrong—she was still beautiful, but something had been lost. Was it that she was no longer a mortal woman with warm skin and a pulse, or had time diluted the love I'd felt for her?

Christian would have given his life for this moment, and the chance to see her again, to speak to her. Life was so ironic. How often did we fail to hold onto what we thought was good for us at the time, only to find in the end that it was not what it seemed?

Josette was here, centuries later, in my club, and all I felt was fear for Amanda and her son who counted on me for protection.

In that moment I realized how much I had changed. I'd grown from a coward into a man, one who knew that others depended on him and that he—I—could not let them down.

"Hello, Michel." She still had a rich French accent, not like mine, which had been diluted after living in New York for a century.

How had she found us? I was afraid to ask, afraid of the answer and wondering why she was here, trying to push open a door I had closed centuries ago.

"Are you surprised to see me?" she said.

Finally, I found my voice. "Quite, Madame Delacore."

Chapter 16
Michel

It was the summer of 1787. We—Christian and I—had been vampires for only thirty years. Josette was a mortal woman, married to a minor aristocrat, Luc Delacore. She had become the mistress of the vampire Gaétan. We had all heard the rumors of her beauty and kindness, but nothing could have prepared us for the reality of that woman.

Christian and I had met Josette with Gaétan one night. She was strolling arm in arm with him on the Pont Neuf. All the rumors were true—she was an exquisite creature—and Christian, speechless around her from the start, may have fallen in love with her in that very first encounter. I must confess that I, too, was smitten.

Not long after, she and Christian had become lovers. Gaétan grew to hate … no, to despise … But no, there really isn't a word for how he felt about Christian, for Christian had stolen Josette away. Gabrielle became angry with Christian, as well, for abandoning her bed for that of a mortal girl—a trollop, I believe, was the word she had used.

It all took place in the early days of La Révolution Française. Paris was frenetic. Things grew tense as the wars of the mortals affected even the undead, dividing us and straining the tenuous, bloody bonds that held us together.

* * *

And here was Josette herself, in my club.

She was draped in a velvet cape that touched the floor. In its folds, she appeared small, almost childlike, though I had always seen her as a powerful seductress.

The vampire beside her, the one who looked so much like Christian that he was a distraction, remained still but studied me carefully, as if he had heard horrible things about me and was trying to discern whether they were true. His hand rested lightly on her shoulder. Was he protecting her? And from what?

Then, slowly, like tumblers falling into place in a lock, I understood. I wasn't sure how it could be possible, but I knew who had sired him.

My face must have given me away.

"Yes, Michel," Josette said gently, "this is Mathieu, Christian's son."

Christ. I made a mental note to apologize to Amanda if I made it home alive tonight. She had been right all along, and I had doubted her.

I tried to still my thoughts, although I had a million questions. Did Christian know of the boy? Where had Mathieu been all this time? An explanation would likely require hours of conversation, and I didn't have hours. Still …

They were waiting. I had to say something.

I swallowed. "I had no idea Christian had a son. Hello, Mathieu."

None of us moved.

"You both left, remember?" Josette smiled, though it never touched her eyes. "Left me in a burning bedroom while you ran to catch a ship to London. I found out, much later, that I was with child … again.

"Michel and your father are dear friends." Josette addressed her son but never lost eye contact with me. "That was the one thing I could always count on. They were inseparable."

I held my tongue. Where would I begin to discuss the past? I had let Josette go a long, long time ago. It had been Christian who had never been able to resolve his feelings for her or to reconcile his guilt over leaving her. Both his confusion and his guilt had weighed against his love for the woman who now stood before me, very much an immortal.

"Inseparable until now, anyway." She smirked at Mathieu, but she spoke now to me. "He left you both, didn't he, to seek me here in Paris? Amanda knew it all along, and now here you both are, and Christian is with his … father."

She knew about Amanda. *Merde.*

"Philippe Du Mauré has been dead for hundreds of years," I whispered.

"True, but Philippe was not Christian's real father. His mother Eléanore bedded a far older and more powerful being and conceived Christian. This was the secret she took to her grave."

"What are you saying? Who is this being of whom you speak?"

"I cannot speak of him, though he always watched over you both, and when I was rotting away in prison, he came to me and offered me immortality in exchange for my son." She nodded towards Mathieu.

And then she began a tale so far-fetched I knew it had to be true. I had lived a long time and had heard all manner of bullshit, but her story chilled me. Mathieu's eyes never left mine as Josette spoke about raising him in the French countryside with a mortal woman named Nell, and about this being … I wasn't even sure she called him by name— perhaps protecting them both, though, why, she would not say.

And this mysterious being was Christian's true father?

I thought back to when Christian's mother had just died. Soon after, we'd stumbled upon a stranger in her boudoir, rummaging through her things.

Could it be … Andreas?

Now I knew why he'd been there. Eléanore had been his lover, and he'd meant to take anything he could by which to remember her.

I drew a long breath. "Where is Christian now, Josette?"

"Somewhere in France."

"And this *being*—Christian's father. Does he have a name?" I did not, in fact, want her to know that he and I had met Andreas several times, the latest having been in our town house in New York City.

She shrugged. "When he came to Eléanore, he was Captain Andreas, so perhaps that is what we should call him."

Another chill went through me. I was right. How often the memory of him rummaging around Christian's house had haunted me. I'd even thought he might have been a dream. "And this—Captain Andreas—does not realize that his son wants nothing more than to be left alone to dwell on his past mistakes?"

"Meaning me?" Josette snapped.

"Christian has never gotten over you, my lady. He is still racked with guilt and pain over … the entire affair."

"And what about you, my dear Michel?"

I swallowed hard. "Forever the *roué*, I suppose."

"A *roué* playing house with a beautiful mortal girl who, I suspect, is not so mortal?"

"She saved Christian's life," I blurted out, focusing on Mathieu. "She was in turn reborn with the blood of another vampire, which gives her vampire … intuitions."

"She has more than that, Michel," Josette said. "I'm not stupid. That so-called mortal is one of my descendants, and you know how powerful I was even before being turned."

I had always wondered. There had been Christian's intense attraction to Amanda, and something about her had reminded him of Josette, too, with blood that had called to him like the song of a siren. Amanda had no notion of her heritage, and now she was even more powerful, full of Sabin's blood.

How ironic, the continuing circle of fate that kept them bound to one another.

Josette and Mathieu's presence was more than unsettling. How long had Amanda been telling me about seeing Christian in the club? Six months, at least, which meant that Josette's presence in California was no coincidence. Her motives could only bode horribly for Amanda and her unborn child.

"Leave us, Mathieu," Josette said. "Wait for me outside."

Obediently, he bled away into the darkness, leaving the two of us alone.

Perhaps I should have had questions, but I had closed the door on Josette centuries ago. While almost impossible to believe she was here, nothing she did should have surprised me. I was no longer in love with her, and in that regard, she had the wrong vampire.

Having watched her son go, Josette turned back to me. "Christian's father sent us here from the New World. There is much unrest and no leadership, and Andreas wants Christian to assume the throne—"

I burst out laughing, so overwhelmed that tears of blood filled my eyes. I tried to catch the blood before it stained my leather jacket. "Josette, that makes no sense. Is this Andreas deluded?"

"He is more powerful than you could ever imagine. He is holding Christian hostage, and he has plans for him. Plans that even I cannot thwart."

Again, I needed to apologize to Amanda. "So, what now? Surely you did not come all this way to return a piece of jewelry I gave you centuries ago."

And then her face changed, and for a moment, she seemed human again, vulnerable and unsure of herself, like the mortal girl I remembered, though a memory shaded in layers of time and history, was not the creature that now stood before me. I had moved forward in time, and it was as if she had no place here in the twenty-first century.

"Remember the last night in the Château des Singes, Michel. Remember—"

"We promised to never, ever talk about it." Though I thought about the events of that night and my part it in every day of my long life, I had never spoken about it to anyone, even her. It was like it had never happened.

"That is where Christian is being held," Josette snapped. "In that godforsaken place."

Dare I believe her? But I did not hesitate. "You seemed to like it when you were sprawled across Monsieur Pilou's bed."

Her hand flew up, but I grabbed it before she could slap me. "Why did you come back here now?" I asked. "You never truly cared about either of us—it was the power, the jewels and castles that lured you. What is left for us to discuss now?"

"Christian needs our help, Michel. We cannot turn our backs on him, despite how he turned his on me."

Poor, poor Josette.

I shook my head. I hated the drama, and wherever Josette Delacore landed, there was always drama.

Vampires were like animals—if you showed fear, you were fucked—so, with all the strength I could muster, I turned my back, left her on the catwalk, and went downstairs and out the rear exit, hoping she would not follow me.

She had been the center of my world for what I'd considered the best years of my young vampire life, yet I was walking away.

Perhaps age does bring wisdom.

I cleared the back door, stepped out into the salt-filled air, and was at our cottage in moments. I cannot fly, but I can move faster than the naked eye when necessary.

Creeping into our cottage, I ran through the tiny living room into our bedroom to find Amanda curled up under the covers of her queen-sized bed. She appeared so tiny and vulnerable. Shit—I had thought we were safe, but no.

We were done here.

PART TWO

Existence, after losing her, would be hell.

Chapter 17
Michel

2010—Le Marais, Paris

Le Marais was once a marsh; hard to imagine now but I could still see the medieval bones of Paris amidst all the twenty-first century trappings. It had evolved into one of the swankest neighborhoods in Paris, with museums, art galleries, and high-end boutiques, reminding me of the West Village in Manhattan. Le Rue des Lions was lined with brownstones like the Upper East Side of Manhattan. It was just perfect.

Amanda and I were out walking one evening when I stopped in front of a three-story mansion. "It reminds me of New York."

"Yes, it certainly does. This house is exquisite." Amanda sighed, all but putty in my hands.

I gestured that she follow me up the walk to the front door. A look of confusion crossed her face when I produced a set of keys. "*Entre*, mademoiselle," I said, handing her the keys.

She beamed as she unlocked the front door. "Oh, Michel." She sighed again, entering the foyer.

Even the layout was similar to that of our brownstone in New York City with two rooms on each floor and two bedrooms occupying the top floor. We had numerous fireplaces and sweeping views of the Seine. The massive front door opened right into a living room with a small dining room behind it. The kitchen and pantry were on the ground floor, with French doors opening onto a walled garden. A run-down shed stood at one end of our property.

At night, the beautifully lit St. Louis en l'Ile was like a beacon from our living room window. It was beautiful and romantic.

Amanda looked so happy. "It's perfect."

* * *

I was happy to be back in Paris and embraced her like a long-lost lover, one who had aged but was beautiful and familiar nonetheless. I thought Amanda and I both felt right at home. The house had an eclectic mix of authentic furniture styles, which for her was familiar, like being back working at the Metropolitan Museum of Art.

Once we settled in, I began to go out at night and leave her alone, searching for anything I could find out about Christian. It sickened me that I had to weigh Amanda's safety against trying to gain information, but I had to act quickly. Once her child came along, I would never be able to leave Amanda's side.

There was no way I would go back to the Château des Singes. I didn't care how many times Amanda bugged me. I had my reasons, and I would just have to lie to her, tell her that I had gone out there and found the house abandoned.

But suppose Christian was being held prisoner there? I mean, suppose Amanda was right? I had learned to trust her psychic abilities, but I could risk neither taking her there nor going back to that place myself.

I tried to put it out of my mind. Christian had abandoned both of us for the memory of Josette Delacore. Quite honestly, maybe he deserved to be locked up for a while. ... *God, he is my best friend, and I hate to feel this way.* I decided I would continue to search for him, but I would not go back to that god-awful place.

I developed a pattern. I would wait until Amanda was asleep then head out for a few hours. I knew no vampire could get into the house without an invitation from Amanda, and her blood made her almost immune to hypnosis from our kind. Whatever the explanation, we vampires could not read her mind.

I had researched all of the clubs and degenerate places our kind would linger, trying to prepare myself, I guess for what I might be walking into by coming back home. Christian had read everything, even *National Geographic* magazine. There had been an article in a long-ago edition about the catacombs of Paris, which I had found interesting because he'd generally avoided anything Parisian. So I'd read the article, which had spoken of the underground tunnels and tours. I could not imagine ever going belowground, but with wine tastings and all sorts of social activities there, I thought, w*hat a perfect place for vampires to linger*—especially those who were more modern in their thinking.

* * *

One night, I crossed into Montparnasse, heading towards the Place Denfert-Rochereau metro stop. The last time I had been here, there had been no museum or metro stop. Paris was almost unrecognizable to me now. The city smelled better than I remembered, and there was so much light. The buildings were still magnificent.

I slipped into the catacomb museum, unnoticed by the smoking and chattering humans grouped out in front. The door was easy to open. Having no interest in the gift shop, I descended the spiral staircase, losing count after one hundred steps. Even for me, the darkness felt claustrophobic. Ignoring the two rooms full of detailed photographs of the tunnels, I continued to follow the winding walls.

Finally, a narrow doorway appeared ahead. There were words etched in the stones. I read them and shivered.

Arrete! C'est isi L'Empire de la Mort.

French for *Stop! Here is The Empire of the Dead.*

I stepped over the threshold into the narrow passage. The stacks of human bones and skulls that lined the walls gave the tunnel a chalky glow. The skulls seemed to laugh at me as I passed, as if saying that all mortals end up in the same place. It got colder as I approached a darker passageway off to the right, and I almost fell into a gaping pit in the floor.

I approached the pit until I could see the metal ladder secured to one side. *Shit, I have to go down there.*

Already my dark clothes were covered in a thin layer of dust. I put one foot and then the other on the metal rungs of the ladder. I held my breath, sensing no one as I descended, counting twenty steps until I felt the floor beneath me.

I was in a cavernous room with a ceiling at least twenty feet off the ground. In one corner was an abandoned truck, stripped of its tires. A wooden table, chairs, and a mound of empty beer cans filled another corner.

Humans actually hung out here? The thought of it almost made me sick.

Lit torches lined the walls. Their flames cast dancing shadows on the floor.

Crazy cataphiles, I thought, scanning the place. Another doorway took me into a smaller but equally well-lit chamber. A rolling wave painted in the Japanese style covered one wall, and in another, even smaller room were a stone table and benches. The smell of burnt wax rose from numerous melted candles stuck to the table.

What did they do down here? I wondered, finding my way back to the large room, where an archway caught my eye. As I moved closer, I smelled something, ever so faint but certainly present.

Blood.

I entered the tunnel and walked through a beautiful Romanesque archway. I began to hear music, very faintly at first. Where there is music, there must be mortals—and vampires.

I picked up my pace and followed the sounds and smells until I found myself at the entrance to another massive cave. Torches strapped to limestone pillars covered in graffiti supported the low ceiling, and the cave was packed with men and women, all clapping their hands and dancing. It was like watching a silent movie, since the stones absorbed the sounds. The cacophony of voices was immediately silenced. There was a time when I would have been among them all, but I was on a mission.

I watched until the bodies parted like the sea, and moving among them, smiling and laughing, danced a beautiful creature who could only be a vampire. He was like the fox in the hen house, surrounded by all the dancing mortals. His coppery red hair flowed down his back in waves, a contrast to his black clothing, which looked rather stylish. I found myself drawn to him, and suddenly, I was moving to the music without thought, releasing tensions and worries to the stone walls that surrounded me.

I had not felt so free in a long time.

A beautiful young woman tried to wrap herself around me, and despite those swirling around the red-haired vampire, his attention was now on me. I smiled and shrugged, knowing how territorial vampires could be. His energy felt old to me, rather like that of Captain Andreas.

He was suddenly in front of me, his green eyes beckoning me. Euphoric, I followed him back towards the tiny room with the stone table and chairs. I knew better than to speak, rather let him lead. After all, this was his territory, and I was an interloper. He could have killed me if he so chose, and there would be nothing I could do about it. I thought about Amanda and how stupid and irresponsible it had been of me to leave her alone with no word as to my whereabouts.

"Please sit down." The vampire motioned towards the stone benches.

I nodded and took a seat facing the doorway, in case I had to attempt to make an escape. Not that I would get far, but I needed at least to feel as if I were in control, even if it were only an illusion. Though he had a French accent, I heard undertones of another language, perhaps Celtic or German, giving his French a more guttural sound. He looked more Germanic, and my thoughts raced over the possibilities of his origins, and his identity.

He sat across from me, resting his folded hands on the table. There was nothing hostile or untoward about him. His green eyes glowed in the torchlight, and it was only then that I saw how similarly we were dressed, as though we read the same fashion magazines. I liked him, despite knowing nothing about him. I felt safe, and I knew somehow that he would not harm me—it was something about the way he looked at me, not as an enemy, but with curiosity and interest.

Much had changed since I'd roamed the streets and catacombs of eighteenth-century Paris, but certain rules still applied, and I thought it best not to keep my host in the dark. I rose, prepared to kneel before him and said, "My name is Michel Baptiste. I am from New York City, recently relocated back to Paris, the city of my birth—"

"Please, remain seated, Michel." The vampire smiled. "I appreciate your politesse, but these are modern times."

I sat back down, grateful not to have to dirty my trousers, though, in truth, there were no "modern times" for vampires. We lived in a world dictated by a strict code of conduct. Being back in Paris had thrust me right into the thick of it again, and I found myself wondering why he was breaking all the rules and throwing etiquette to the wind. What need did he have that outweighed the protocol that held our society together?

"I'm Victor." He extended his hand. "I spend most of my time here in the catacombs."

I was floored. His behavior was so mortal, so casual and out of character. A vampire would never, ever have made so human a gesture, but I was forced to comply, so I reached across the table and shook his hand. It was surprisingly warm for that of a vampire.

"I gather that it has been quite some time since you have visited the catacombs," he said.

"Yes." I folded my hands in my lap in a show of submission. "Two hundred and twenty-six years, to be exact. I am surprised to see so many mortals cavorting down here."

"Oh, yes, they have wine tastings, poetry readings— it's quite civilized."

Although I could think of other words to describe their behavior, I said nothing.

His smile widened. "But," he said precisely, "that is not why you are here."

His candor alarmed me—again, nothing like that of a typical vampire, which would have been nothing if not vague and indirect.

"No, it is not." I pushed a curl away from my face, unsure of how much to tell him. I thought that his demeanor warranted the courtesy of an honest answer. "I am looking for a friend who came to Paris recently. I … He … We had lived together in New York for more than one hundred years when he quite suddenly decided to come back here. Now he does not answer my calls or my texts. I thought perhaps that, by coming here, I might at least meet a vampire who had seen him or heard something about him."

"Perhaps your friend does not want to be found." He leaned forward, and I sensed he knew more than he would say. Perhaps he had even met Christian or at least heard about him.

"You may be right." Who was I fooling? If Christian had wanted to make contact, he would have done so already. I was like Don Quixote, chasing windmills. Nevertheless … "My friend is nothing if not stubborn. Once he gets something in his head, there is no persuading him otherwise."

"Does your friend have a name?"

"Christian … Christian Du Mauré."

I could have sworn Victor's posture shifted. I continued, pretending not to have noticed. "He is as tall as I am, with flowing blond hair and dark eyes. He scowls often. Believe me, if you had met him, you would not soon forget him. He's hard to miss."

"Du Mauré …" Victor scratched his head. Either the gesture was sincere, or he was putting on a show of interest to win me over.

I waited for the tumblers to click into place. Every vampire in Paris knew who we were; we were legends among our kind, for we had defied our maker and used violence to secure our freedom. No vampire had ever turned on its maker nor had ever requested permission to leave their maker's side and survived, and we had done both—quite successfully, I might have added.

At any rate, we were infamous, and there were vampires who found our conduct reprehensible and would kill either of us on sight. It was the risk I took by coming back, but Christian was worth the risk, and I was hoping that my newfound friend Victor was not one of those vampires with a conscience and an attachment to the old ways, despite his modern behavior.

I knew it was best to say nothing. Victor would come to his own conclusions. Once again, I regretted my stupidity in going to the catacombs. Not for me, mind you—I could handle whatever Victor had in mind, and I had lived a long and adventurous life—but Amanda filled my thoughts, alone and defenseless against such supernatural forces. I had vowed to protect her, and if I did not return home, what then?

Finally, Victor folded his arms. "Tell me why you fled Paris. I wish to hear it from you, not the rumors that have been swilling around this city for centuries."

I had no choice but to give him the history of Christian's and my relationship with Gabrielle, our maker. I told Victor about meeting Josette Delacore and stealing her away from Gaétan. Before long, he'd heard an abbreviated, but just as sordid, tale of the five of us and how it had become unbearable to remain together. I explained how Christian had grown to hate Gabrielle for turning me, giving him no choice but to join us.

Victor leaned back. "And this woman, Josette Delacore—what became of her?"

"She was made vampire centuries ago, and she is out for revenge. We would not turn her, despite her pleas."

"Hell hath no fury like a woman scorned, they say." Victor shrugged. "Though, if your friend Christian looks anything like you, I can understand the lady's wrath."

I was unsure what to say. I did not feel as though he were making overtures towards me. No, he liked women far too much, but he was being brutally honest. "Even vampires must move on, Victor." *Easier said than done.*

"You have nothing to fear from me, Michel. But there are those among us who are less … forward-thinking." He stood slowly and that was my cue that this conversation was over. "If I ever hear anything about your friend, or happen to run into him, how might I contact you?"

"Just text me," I said, prepared to give him my cell phone number.

He shook his head—"I abhor modern technology"—I chose not to give him my address, not with Amanda there, so I shrugged, saying nothing.

When he extended his hand, I took it willingly, though I wondered whether his curiosity or his fear would get the better of him and he would follow me home.

As I made my way home that night, I wondered if meeting him would backfire on Amanda and me.

If I were him, I would definitely not let this opportunity escape and I would follow me.

Either way, I imagined that our paths would cross again.

Chapter 18
Amanda

2010—Le Marais, Paris

Michel and I only ever speak of our fears when we're wrapped around one another in the darkness at night. He never told me why we fled California for Paris so quickly, and I did not—even now, do not—ask. We want to find Christian, and Paris seemed like the logical place to begin our search, but my hopes were dashed early on.

Michel confessed that he went to the Château des Singes—alone, of course. He would not have risked taking me along. Though I understand his point of view, I wanted to see it for myself.

I do believe him when he describes the condition of the house and adds that no one, human or vampire, could possibly live there.

Still, I wonder ... my dreams of Christian being there. How could I have gotten it so wrong?

* * *

I become the day-time shopping maven of the Marais. Before long, I know every *boulangerie*, bookstore, food market, and second-hand store for blocks.

But once the sun sets, I become a shut-in, albeit in the most beautiful surroundings imaginable.

Although it remains unspoken, I know that Michel is still searching for Christian. I wish I could join him, but I have a major handicap—my mortality.

Many nights, we sit by the fire and just talk. All we have, after all, is each other. His stories of his youth enthrall me. He talks about the Louvre when it was still a palace, and how Paris was buzzing with change. There were no middle class, women's rights, children's health care, or a voice for the common man.

Looking back at the history of Paris, I even grow to understand the whys of the French Revolution. Michel speaks of Paris, of the city in total chaos, filled with bloodshed and fear. You could pluck it out of the air, it hung so heavily, he says.

Back then, he wore the finest lace blouses, buckled shoes, and silk trousers. He and Christian were immune to guilt or worry, having only to drink and fornicate and linger in the salons of mortals, playing card games and gambling while they chattered on and on, debating ideas, eating and drinking their lives away.

And all the while, the guillotine lay in wait like a jealous lover.

Now, as then, the Seine slithers through the streets like an onyx snake. One evening, while we stand talking on the Pont Neuf, Michel expresses feeling at once calm and excited, but also incredibly sad and adrift, and so very alone. My heart breaks for him.

Dare I tell him I feel exactly the same way?

We never talk about the Château des Singes until one night, when I almost convince him to rent a car and drive me out to the abandoned château just so I can take a look at it. I would drive, I explain, and I promise to stay in the car while he looks around again—it makes perfect sense.

Instead, he dismisses the plan, calling it crazy.

* * *

Four days later, we sit by the fire talking about the summer when the three of them—Christian, Michel, and Josette—met. Michel becomes silent, and his silence seems to go on forever as he stares deeper into the fire. His profile still takes my breath away.

My heart beats in my throat. *Why is he suddenly reticent?*

"I have not been totally forthcoming with you," he whispers to the roaring fire. "I told you that once I showed Christian Josette's death certificate, and that the finality of her death turned him into a wild beast who slaughtered indiscriminately, without reason or judgment. My life-long friend who had seemed to cringe at the thought of taking human blood had become a madman, who risked exposing both of us on more than one occasion."

Michel turns towards me, his light eyes hidden in half-shadows. "That was not entirely true." He touches my arm as if he needs assurance. "I desperately wanted to be with Josette again, alone without Christian hovering around us constantly, like a fly on a hot summer night. Perhaps I still was in love with her, or only thought I was in love with her. The reasons no longer matter."

I nod once, yet I dare not judge, for I want him to continue. I'll never hear enough about the three of them.

"One night," he goes on, "as I came home in the usual pre-dawn hours, I noticed a note on our stone steps. I would have walked right over it except for the black sealing wax. Although it was brief, I immediately recognized the handwriting. Josette had fled Paris for London, wondering if we were still there. The year was 1810, of course, and we had been living in London since July of 1790."

"Michel, how did she find you?"

"How did she do anything?" He shrugs. "She was so powerful. … It's hard to explain."

"I thought she was imprisoned. Or was that a ruse, too?"

He looks at me and smiles. "She had been imprisoned, and I calculated that she would be thirty-eight years old by then. God knew what shape she'd be in, but I knew I had to see her, and yet I could not risk Christian ever knowing about it."

"And so you locked Christian away, pretending he had gone mad so you could see her?" I recoil from him. How could he do that to his best friend?

Michel pauses. "He *was* mad, Amanda. I did the only thing I could think of to protect us both ... but yes, I was desperate to see her, and I used his madness as justification to lock him away. There was, however, so much more."

I hold my breath, waiting for him to continue.

"One night, as I was preparing to go out, the doorbell rang. No one had ever rung our bell before, and only one person would have made such an entrance. When I opened the door, there she stood, exactly as I had remembered her on the sweltering July night we'd met in the summer of 1787. She was still fifteen years old."

"But I though you said she was thirty-eight years—" I stop. At this moment, I hate him and want to cause him pain, because I know where this story is going. He withheld this from Christian. What kind of friend was he? He was a sneak and a liar ... and yet, he is my lifeline, and my only hope, at the moment.

Michel puts his hand on my knee as if anchoring himself to me. "Josette had been made vampire in prison in 1793. She never revealed the circumstances that forced her to leave France and come in search of us in London.

"I told her about Christian and what I had done to protect him from himself, how I feared for his eternal soul and his fragile life. I knew she understood my reasons, but she had no way of knowing that when she showed up on our doorstep."

"Or so you wanted to believe? She might have been in London longer than you imagined, stalking you both."

"I believe she came looking for us. She was concerned about Christian and understood my sense of relief—"

"Relief?" I ask. "What the hell do you mean by relief?"

Michel looks away. "I left him locked away for too many years while I cavorted with her. I finally felt free of him, if only for a short while. He had become a monster, and I'd been so torn ... but now I could be on my own and have her all to myself." He runs his hand through his dark curls.

I say nothing, not sure what I feel. Disgust, sadness, anger. I try to put myself in his shoes and imagine the love triangle through his eyes. Though he always downplayed his relationship with Josette Delacore, I know how much he loved her. I see how that was a second chance for them both.

"I loved her without reason," Michel says, "and I had had to deny it for so long to my best friend as we three had danced around one another, but now I could truly love her and be myself without reproach or censure, without wondering when her husband or Christian would stumble upon us. No more sneaking around or lying to one another."

I must look surprised.

He confesses, "It was the best thirty years of my life, Amanda. But like all good things, it had to end."

After a pause, Michel continues. "You know, from the moment she stepped back into my life, I felt tremendous guilt. She had lost her son and was riddled with guilt and angst."

"She had a son? I knew about Solange, her daughter with you, but another child?"

"Yes, she had a son while she was in prison. His name was Mathieu, born in April 1791. She knew of a French family who was able to get him out just as Christian had gotten Solange out of Paris the year before. She had Mathieu whisked away to London just after he was born to save him from a most certain death. She was made vampire in prison two years later.

"I know what you're thinking," he adds. "It sounds crazy, but I believed her. She was a vampire, still young and beautiful, but she was not the same woman I had known years earlier."

My mind is racing. "Michel, I have a million questions, but the most obvious one is, who was the father of her child?"

"Christian."

The ground seems to shift under my feet. I remember the diary that I touched in my office at the Met, and the images it conjured up for me, of Josette with the little boy with the dark eyes and blond curls. That was Christian's son?

Michel stammers, "Yes, she had been pregnant when we three said our good-byes, but even she had not known it."

"So you both had no idea when you fled Paris?"

"No, no. By 1840, my guilt had become too much to bear, and Josette was becoming restless. She had resolved some of her grief over losing Mathieu, and I believe we both realized that love does not conquer all. She bid me good-bye, and I went about freeing my best friend. London had grown incredibly dull by this time."

My entire body deflates with disappointment.

"I can see the look in your eyes," Michel says. "You think I am a monster, no?"

My stomach flips as I shake my head. "I'm not sure how I feel right now."

"I have told no one about this, Amanda. I trust you, and I know you love Christian. With that love, you must understand that if you ever see Christian again, he must never know about any of it."

"How did... Mathieu ... die?" I ask.

"Josette told me he was murdered by a vampire, but she would disclose no more than that."

"My God, who hated her enough to murder her son? I mean, that is the ultimate revenge, isn't it?" I watch Michel. What might he do to me when he grows bored and no longer wants the responsibility of me and my child? Will he lock me away, too?

Late that night, I dream of being buried alive, and wake screaming, sweat pouring off my face and blood pooling on the mattress.

Chapter 19
Josette

2010—Venice Beach, California

My confrontation with Michel had been disastrous. I had thought he would be happy to see me, but in truth his reaction had been quite the opposite. It had been centuries since we had been together, and, although we had had the most passionate of love affairs, I knew he no longer loved me—if he ever *had* loved me. He wanted only one person—Christian Du Mauré—and if Christian had been so inclined, they would have been lovers, sharing their blood and bed for all eternity.

But Christian had had no such inclinations.

He was loyal, responsible, and faithful, traits I admired and needed in a man, yet which totally eluded me. I, personally, was nothing if not fickle, though I had hidden it well from him. How could I not? Christian had been like a puppy dog at my feet. He would have done anything for me—except make me immortal.

He was, in fact, the only vampire I ever met that abhorred what he was. Once the bloom of his youth had passed and he'd no longer needed to take out his anger on the mere mortals around him, he'd almost detested the taking of blood. When I had known him in Paris, those three years we had been together, he'd been a dignified monster that roamed the filthy streets of Paris with his best friend, looking for victims to satisfy an urge that could never be satisfied.

Michel, on the other hand, was a vampire of a different color. The Michel I had known had been a *roué*, and if I had not seen it with my own eyes, I would not have believed the man he had become.

I had been coming to Michel's for some time now, sometimes alone and sometimes sending Mathieu to spy on him. I had even sat next to Amanda at the bar one night, dressed in leather and a blonde wig. I had tried to make conversation with her, but she'd been distracted by Michel. Oh, she was polite, but she'd had no interest in talking to me.

I could not have said that I blamed her. If the truth were told, I actually found myself envious of her. I don't believe she even realized the hold she had over him. She did not intentionally try to control him, but I knew Michel, and as I watched him make drinks and chat with the women who swooned over him, there was only one woman for him.

Amanda.

This was a Michel I had never seen.

As I'd pretended to sip my glass of Merlot, I had watched him watch her, and I knew that he was not acting the part to appease Christian's memory.

No, he loved the girl.

Then the rest of the truth had overwhelmed me.

How could Amanda not see that her child was Michel's? Was she that stupid?

Christian had not been able to have children, even with me. He'd thought Mathieu was his son because I had told him so. I had wanted to believe it, as well, but finding a mortal man who looked eerily like Christian to impregnate me had been so easy.

So many lies.

Michel, though … He was the key to the prophecy foretold by the Ancient Ones. He carried the seed that could impregnate mortal women.

I didn't believe that Ghislain, or any of the other Ancient beings, with their intelligence and powers far beyond mine, had any idea that Michel was the key, the vampire they should have slaughtered centuries ago if they had truly believed in the prophecy.

Ghislain had it all wrong. Michel was magic in that his seed could create life. How it was possible, I did not know, but Solange, and now Amanda's child, were proof that he was the one who could father children.

I had toyed with the thought of telling him when we met on the catwalk, but would he have believed anything I told him? I should have known that his impulse to protect Amanda and her son would take over. They would surely be gone within days, and I would follow them back to Paris where this little play would unspool one more time.

As I stood at the windows overlooking the Pacific Ocean, I thought about what a farce my life had been, how I had fooled mortals and vampires alike. Was I the parlor trick girl, Beatrice's daughter, pulling tarot cards for desperate patrons who wanted to know if they would be rich or fall in love? I always thought them the poor souls—but was I really any better?

I believed that I had powerful blood, but in terms of siring the Second Coming—no. I had failed miserably.

Though I would always be young and beautiful, I had no real power other than my beauty.

I noticed Sarah running up the winding driveway. It was almost sunrise, and I sensed immediately that it was not good news she was desperate to tell me. Mathieu plodded along behind her.

I put my back to the windows, feeling the morning sun slowly rising. My hands were already clenched in rage, for somehow I knew before Sarah flopped down on the couch what she was going to say.

"They're gone."

Mathieu entered behind her. "All their personal effects are gone, Mother. What happened at the club?"

I fought to remain calm. "Nothing, Mathieu. We spoke, Michel turned to go, and I left, as well. Nothing out of the ordinary was said—"

"He's no dummy, Mother. He knew you would go after the girl. I told you not to show yourself to him."

"Where would they go?" Sarah whispered. I could hear relief in her voice, and although I wanted to be angry with her, I could not hold it against her. She was human. The qualities that had made me gravitate to her were the very qualities that made her so warm and caring. I truly envied the girl.

"Paris, of course." I nodded. "We pack and travel home."

"What about Ghislain? He had ordered us to remain in Paris, and we disobeyed him. Now we have to face him again." Mathieu ran a hand through his blond curls.

I had no answer. To be honest, I was glad to go home. I was not a California girl by any stretch, though I would miss the beauty of the ocean.

"Where shall I look?" Sarah asked.

"Pick a quiet neighborhood with mansions for rent. Le Marais is still more eighteenth-century than modern. Why not try there?" It was worth a look.

"Le Marais, it is." Sarah forced a smile.

As I packed the small steamer trunk I always took with me, I noticed one of my ancient diaries. I sat down on the bed, opened the diary, and began to read.

~

Paris, 1787

*They flowed out of the heat, detaching themselves
from the shadows on a tepid summer night in the year of our
Lord 1787. I was but a girl of fifteen, yet had already been
deflowered by one of the most powerful vampires in all of
Paris, to whose arm I gently clung. I was months away from
marrying a much older man, but at that moment, as the
strangers approached us, Gaétan shifted slightly in front of
me, as if to shield me from them.*

But I was already transfixed.

*Both were tall, well over six feet, and thin, but that is
where any comparison ended, for they were opposites in
appearance and—I would later learn—in almost everything
else under the sun ... or should I say the night sky?*

It was obvious that my lover Gaétan knew them.

*When the tall, blond vampire took my hand and
pressed his cold lips to my skin, I shuddered and shattered,
all in an instant. Perhaps if they had both just kept walking
by, my life would have turned out differently, but I had
begged an introduction, and when his dark eyes locked with
mine, I felt myself exposed, as if a locked door within my
heart had flown open and my soul lay bare for him.*

*When he told me his name—Christian Du Mauré—
his voice curled around me like my favorite silk scarf, and,
although I did not know it then, I had fallen into a chasm I
had no hope of escaping.*

*I braced myself as he explained to Gaétan why he
and his companion were not with Gabrielle, which made my
heart sink for an instant. I sensed that Gaétan could not wait
to whisk me away, but I would have none of it. I could not let
this tall stranger slip away.*

*Then I turned my attention to his friend: Michel
Baptiste. I fought to keep up the pretense that we had never
met, despite the memory of our night spent together last*

*winter at the Château des Singes. Thank goodness it was
dark, for I felt myself blushing.*

*Michel was a human sculpture come to life, with
flowing black hair that caressed high cheekbones and full
lips. His eyes glistened in the torchlight, and though I could
tell they were light, only later would I discover they were
almost a Peridot green, like a stained-glass window with
light shining through.*

*I was so taken with both of them I could barely
breathe. Their energy embraced me, and they captivated me.*

*I would become the wife of Luc Delacore, a wealthy
minor aristocrat to whom my mother had secured a marriage
contract for me when she found out she was dying. It was
either marry Luc or be destitute, and I could no more
stomach a life of poverty than I could fly. I had agreed.*

*I was already Gaétan's lover. He was more than
generous with his gifts, and I was willing to give him
anything in return in the hope that one day he would make
me immortal. So went our dance, and I'd thought it would go
on forever.*

*It might have, until that night, when my life fell apart
and reconstructed itself all at once.*

* * *

*I did not consciously set out to seduce and fall in love
with both Christian and Michel, nor did they glamour me,
for I was beyond hypnosis. Each had what the other lacked. I
found them both intoxicating and as integral to me as
sunshine and fresh air.*

*I could not live without them, yet I could not see what
was to come, despite my clairvoyant abilities, my power to
touch objects and watch, images and feelings running
through me like water. I possessed the gift of psychometry,
yet I had also read tarot cards to entertain my mother's
friends at her numerous parties.*

*Of course she'd had no idea that "Monsieur
Richard," as he'd called himself, was an ancient vampire*

who could have snapped both our necks and left us in ruin if he'd so desired. He'd promised me immortality if I gave him what he desired: my blood. He'd come to my bedroom one night, and while he took both my virginity and my blood, he left me weakened but ecstatic and filled with dreams of power and riches. He'd showered me with clothing and jewels and took me everywhere in Paris ... and all he wanted in return was to drink my blood. He spoke of its power over him.

I was never afraid, quite the contrary. I loved the world of the vampire. It was both silent and powerful, mysterious and glamorous, fraught with drama. I possessed what they wanted—blood, beauty, and a willingness to submit to them. All of them.

I had power, money, and all a woman could ever want, and with Christian and Michel, I felt that our lives were perfect and that we would never cease to be together.

Chapter 20
Josette

2010—Paris

For weeks, I combed the streets of Paris, sometimes alone, sometimes with Mathieu, looking for signs of Michel and Amanda. The city was not as I remembered it, but what was?

The noise bothered me the most, I think. The noise and the lights. Garish skyscrapers had replaced the rolling green hills that had blanketed the Seine, and the Louvre was no longer the largest building in an otherwise empty landscape. Paris had had a smell back in the eighteenth century: mud, excrement, the sound of horses clopping through the narrow streets of Paris. That was what I remembered of my home city. Now it was a cacophony of sounds and car exhaust created by frenetic humans driving cars or riding buses. They moved through their city like buzzing flies.

Even the woods where I had lived were noisy and full of people.

When Mathieu was murdered, I'd had to leave France. It had been part of my bargain with Ghislain. I had agreed yet my grief over losing him left me vulnerable. I'd had to move on, and so I had settled in Canada for a time, but Paris had always been home.

Mathieu, Sarah, and I found a comfortable mansion in the Marais. We settled into a routine, and Mathieu and Sarah began what seemed like a daunting task. Mathieu roamed the endless avenues at night. Sarah frequented bookstores and museums, places she thought Amanda might gravitate towards.

The search was not going well until one day Sarah burst through the front door. "I saw her," she cried, panting.

A frisson of emotion, undeniable, went up my spine. "Here, sit here." I gestured to the space beside me on the couch.

Sarah obeyed and took a long breath. "She lives literally two blocks away. I was walking home when I saw a woman leaving a drugstore. At first, I thought I was imagining the resemblance because I wanted so badly to find her. I followed her, and I am ninety-nine percent positive it's her. She entered a gorgeous mansion on the Rue des Lions."

I drew her close and hugged her. Long gone were the days when I had wanted the release of sex to satisfy unresolved feelings, but I had always enjoyed the warmth of human contact, and Sarah came to me willingly, just as she always had. Her blue eyes brightened when I brushed a strand of hair from her face. "Good work, my love."

Her warm lips were on mine before I could protest, needing from me what I could not give her at that moment— her own release. She fought to draw me into more than an embrace, but all I could think about was Amanda and the child, right on our doorstep. It was too perfect for words. Le Marais was perfect for a young family: quiet, historic, and set apart from the bustle of the city. An eighteenth-century enclave smack in the middle of one of the busiest cities in the world.

* * *

The March wind seemed to carry me along as I made my way through the narrow, winding streets towards the Rue des Lions. It was late, and I passed no one, not that they would have seen me. I was a vampire. Most people did not believe we existed, and I had learned centuries ago how to navigate the shadows and blend with the darkness, drawing it around me like another cape to protect me from the mortals who would have done me harm. Some of the winding streets were so narrow, I couldn't imagine that much sunlight pierced the shadows. At this hour, the only light came from the gaslights along the cobblestone streets.

I approached the address slowly, and from across the street. The elegant, stately mansions had a history all their own. Lost in thought, I almost passed by my intended destination.

It was a three-story mansion on a street with similar houses. Theirs had a small front porch littered with plants and a wooden rocking chair, which I imagined Amanda used during the day.

A low brick wall surrounded the house, separating it from the sidewalk. I hopped the wall and went around back, where I found myself on a grass lawn, staring at French doors that probably led into a kitchen. The faint scent of flowers and freshly turned earth filled my senses. A tiny shed stood at one end of the property, though I sensed no one there.

I sensed no one, mortal or vampire, anywhere, in fact, and so I pressed myself against the brick wall alongside the French doors and peeked around the corner, scanning the kitchen. It was modern, a normal mortal's kitchen, with baby bottles on the counter, a fruit bowl—homey. The house was dark, and I dared not venture up the trellis, but I was tempted. I assumed that Amanda was asleep inside and that Michel was out on the prowl.

I lingered, though I was not sure why. What was I hoping to see?

Then, just as I turned to leave, an arc of light appeared. I ducked aside and looked back.

A refrigerator door had been opened inside. A woman stood there, bathed in the light, wearing a flowing robe that fell to the floor. She was staring into the refrigerator as if she had lost something and thought it might have turned up there. She held a sleeping child—*hers*—on her left hip.

So she has already given birth.

Amanda grabbed a small container of something and a spoon. She was barely awake, her heartbeat slow and mesmerizing. How had I not sensed their presence before?

Not for the first time, I was struck by the similarities between Amanda Perretti and me. We were both petite and dark-haired … but she seemed so vulnerable, so unaware of her beauty, whereas I used mine whenever possible, to manipulate men and vampires alike. Had I ever been as vulnerable as she?

She had an innocence about her. I could see why Michel would want to protect her. Had I mistakenly missed his presence, as well? Was he, too, nearby?

Amanda ate what I guessed was a yogurt, staring as though lost in thought, then dropped the container in the sink and sat down, opening her robe. Her child nuzzled against one engorged breast. She stroked his head as he nursed almost violently.

I thought back to all the times I had nursed a child, first Solange and then Mathieu. When each of my children had been born, there was a slim chance of them living through infancy. Even giving birth had been a risk, and yet, nursing them had grounded me.

I had to admit, it was beautiful to watch Amanda with her son, but as I did so, I grew sadder and sadder. She had something I could never have again: a child. The intimacy of moments such as the one I now witnessed made me feel old and useless. All the feelings of being discarded by both Christian and Michel rose to the surface. I wanted to strike back at the only things Michel loved: this mortal girl and her son.

Now that I knew where they lived, there was time to plan, and it would be easy. So many scenarios filled my mind, arousing me. I imagined how I would kill her slowly, taking back the powerful blood that filled her lithe body, but only after she'd watched me drink her son dry until he shriveled and fell like an empty husk at her feet. Her screams would fill my soul as she begged for both their lives, but it would be futile, for I would take from them what I could never have. Suddenly I felt overjoyed, with a sense of purpose I had not known in decades.

I was about to leave, still ruminating over their demise and my triumph, when I felt something on the street, coming towards the house. I wrapped my cloak more tightly around me and waited. The energy felt vampire, but older and more powerful.

I ran towards the dilapidated shed and tried the rusted door handle, which opened easily. Tools I could not identify rested against the back wall. The shed smelled of wood and mildew, and cobwebs hung everywhere. Through a gap in the wooden door, I could still see Amanda in her kitchen, unaware that she was being watched not by one but two vampires. How very ironic. Was she really so clueless?

She shifted her child from one breast to the other and sat back while he drank.

The other being materialized on the grass. He looked around, sniffing the air as vampires sometimes do, in search of the scent of another of their own kind. If he found me …

But he barely glanced at the shed, and focused instead on Amanda. He seemed entranced by her, even though he had to have smelled me.

I could see a little of his profile, despite the darkness. Had he been here before? Who was he? Did Michel know about him?

I could not take my eyes off him. It was not that he was handsome but that the expression on his face was one of desire, tempered with curiosity. He was of medium height, with flowing auburn hair. He was dressed very much like Michel, in dark, exotic clothing, as if the accoutrements of the modern world could not hide the fact that he was an older being.

Was it a coincidence that we were both here, on the same street in Paris, curious and aroused by the same mortal girl with her powerful blood?

I stepped back and brushed up against one of the tools. It scraped against another. I grabbed it before it could fall, and waited, frozen, to be discovered. Nothing happened.

A long moment later, I went back to the little hole. The vampire had remained where he was, still watching.

Then a shadow crossed Amanda's path inside. Michel entered the kitchen and sat down beside her.

Did he not sense the presence of two vampires literally in his back yard?

When he kissed the infant on the head, I knew that after centuries of debauchery and endless conquests, he had fallen in love with his best friend's woman, just as he had done with me centuries before. We were on a continuous loop that kept repeating over and over.

They both smiled down at the child, who had let go, perhaps having drifted off to sleep. When Michel took the child into his arms and helped Amanda upstairs, I had only to imagine what might transpire between them.

I waited a few moments after the other vampire left. Then, I slowly opened the shed door and crept out of the yard.

As I walked home, down empty streets filled with darkened houses, I fought tears, mourning opportunities long gone, never to be recaptured.

Chapter 21
Amanda

2011—Paris

We've been living in the Marais for close to a year. Michel and I have settled into a routine. I go out only during the day, taking Julien with me, while Michel rests in the darkness that consumes him. Around dinnertime, he emerges and joins us in our elegant Louis XVI-era dining room. The house came furnished, though he still will not reveal the source of all of the incredible antiques.

It still pains me to think that his and Christian's town house in New York burned to the ground with all of the history they had amassed there since moving to New York in 1901. I wonder if Christian knows that his precious antiques and books are lost forever. That someone wanted both of them either dead, or at least unable to remain in New York. Who would do such a thing? Despite my suspicions, I can't draw any definite conclusions, and I have Julien to occupy me.

It is impossible not to love my son. What mother does not love the child she created and brought into the world? Yet what nags at the back of my mind is a simple yet incredibly complex and confusing question.

Who is Julien's father?

He was born on New Year's Eve, 2010, delivered by Michel in a flurry of screams and much blood. He was strong and took to my breast immediately. Michel and I both laughed and cried at our accomplishment. I think I slept for two days straight after the birth.

Julien has dark hair and eyes, soulful ancient eyes, but it's still too soon to tell his parentage.

I felt at first that it could be none other than Christian, and I took such joy in knowing that I had been able to give him a son … but what if this child was fathered by his enemy, and my one-night stand, Gaétan? I can't see much of a resemblance between Julien and Christian. Yet Michel speaks of him as Christian's son, so I keep putting the question out of my mind and believe as hard as I can that Christian really *is* my son's father.

Even if Julien isn't Christian's child, I love him no less … but it makes the question of his parentage even more complicated.

The world of the Parisian vampires is a complex one, and once I found out I was pregnant, my only concern was for my child's well-being. The ancient rivalries and struggles were overwhelming, and yet I knew how real they were. I tried not to go back to the night on the rooftop of the Grey Wolf when Christian lay dying, almost cut in two by his vampire daughter, Solange, and how I had saved him with my magical blood.

I almost died myself, yet I was given the blood of another vampire and survived, only to be changed in ways that were subtle. I have acute hearing and smell. My gift of psychometry is heightened. I'm careful what I touch, for images assail me, and like a movie playing out, I hear and see things associated with the object at hand. I sometimes wonder how I can ever go back to work in a museum again. How can I handle objects and explain how I know what I know about a piece?

In touching the portrait of Josette Delacore in Christian's boudoir, I saw her with Gaétan, the person I knew as Thomas, the night guard at the Metropolitan Museum of Art. His intentions passed through me, and I suddenly knew who he really was, and that his purpose in coming to New York was to slaughter me, but that he'd grown greedy and wanted me, and my blood, for himself.

Then, innocently, I touched a diary, only to see images of Josette Delacore again, and I knew that she hadn't died but had been made vampire. Christian knew, too, but never told us. I'm convinced that that was why he fled New York for Paris: to find her, or to finally put to rest his obsession with her.

I'm still trying to live with the knowledge that he loved her more than anything and anyone, except Michel. Josette was Christian's world, and the best years of his vampiric life were when they were together. Although it was only a brief three years, they were the highlight of his long life.

I feel so sorry for him. He was chasing a ghost who proved to be no ghost at all, but a woman who got what she wanted and became immortal. She can only be here in France. This was her home, and I know Christian found her.

Michel and I were living so peacefully in Venice Beach, in a cottage by the sea, seemingly so far away from this world. I thought we were safe, but one night, he came home, his light green eyes darkened in fear, and I knew we had to leave the United States. He never told me why, just that we were no longer safe there.

Since then, I have grown to trust Michel as I once trusted Christian, and perhaps even more so, for Michel would never abandon me like Christian did so readily.

Michel goes out every night, probably still searching for Christian, or perhaps for a vampire whom they knew back in the eighteenth century, someone familiar to reconnect with. Or maybe he wants to be among his own kind, now that Christian is gone. Does Michel feel somewhat responsible for Christian's behavior? He'll never admit it. Guilt is not in Michel's repertoire of emotions. He says even less about his predatory adventures. Paris was, and is, his world, so I trust him to keep us safe, and he has promised he will, at all costs.

Usually he sits with us while I eat meals and feed Julien. Then I bathe my son and put him to bed. Once I retire for the evening, Michel leaves us. Sometimes he goes out early and returns home just as I'm going up to bed. It must be a tough balancing act.

I love Michel for his loyalty to Christian, which extends to Julien and me. Michel's *joie de vivre* is contagious, even in this difficult time. I guess it's always been his way.

When I reflect on Christian and me as a couple, Michel and I are more serious and pragmatic, by comparison, though sometimes I wonder if Michel's cavalier attitude in all things is a ruse and he's just as vulnerable and scared as the rest of us. Perhaps he's even more pragmatic than I am, having lived for over two hundred and fifty years. Nothing much seems to shock or scare him. He's seen all matter of human nature and lived through things I only read about. Sometimes, we sit together and talk about his life, whether it was his youth spent in France, his flight to London during the French Revolution, or his life in the American West for a period of time. I was never sure how Christian and Michel ended up in Northern California, but there they lived for sixty years before migrating to Manhattan in 1901.

* * *

One fall evening, I bathe and nurse Julien and put him to bed right after dinner. He seems out of sorts, but as soon as I put him in his crib and cover him with his favorite blanket, he's asleep. I hear Michel in the bathtub and assume he's preparing for a night out.

I'm settled in front of the fire with a hot cup of tea and the latest John Connolly novel when I feel him near me.

"Hot date tonight?" I smile, putting the book down

"Do you like it?" He pivots in a pair of black leggings, a sheer black tunic that falls to just below his waist, and leather boots that hug his thighs. He wears several silver chains and numerous bracelets. His hair is blown out, making his usual curls subtler.

"Let me guess—a date with Anna Wintour?"

He crosses his arms and scowls. "Perish the thought."

"Seriously, you look beautiful, as always, Michel. Who is she?"

He shakes his head vehemently. "I'm vampire bait, my love."

I know exactly what he means. Michel always dresses as exotically as possible to visit clubs. Even at home he isn't a jeans-and-T-shirt kind of guy. He looks ravishing in a Goth sort of way.

He's trying to find out anything he can about Christian, which means hitting all the clubs and dark places vampires meet up these days. Gone are the days of the French court where he and Christian found themselves with a plethora of mortals to choose from. Even the Pont Neuf is tame now, well-lit and policed through the wee hours of the morning.

I walk him to the front door where he quickly kisses my cheek, whispering, "Call me." It's his catchphrase. He knows the risk of leaving me unattended but needs to go.

I kiss his cheek, cold from lack of feeding, and smile into his light eyes. "Thank you, Michel."

Pushing the lace curtain aside, I watch him descend the front steps and melt into the shadows on the street, a wisp devoured by the darkness just outside the front porch light. I wait there, taking in the shadows and the beautiful mansions on our street where few cars travel and even fewer people pass. Most Parisians are already home from work, preparing for their late dinners and settling in for the evening.

I try to imagine the clubs Michel visits, but his world here is so unfamiliar to me. I keep telling myself he knows what he's doing, but worry always nags in the back of my mind.

What if he doesn't come home?

One of his and Christian's best friends, Sabin, left for Paris over a year ago to find lodgings for us. We never heard from him again. Michel never mentions him, but we both sense that something happened.

Then there's Gabrielle, who also left New York for Paris, just as Sabin did, and who, as far as I know, also vanished. If Michel has been in touch with her, he hasn't shared it with me. Perhaps the less I know right now, the better. I have Julien to think about and care for. At a year old, he's walking, and so much more demanding than when he was an infant.

I've started my search for a housekeeper, though I hesitate to bring any mortal into our home. It's so risky. Still, I need help.

I haven't broached the subject with Michel. I know what he'll say.

Saving that conversation for another night, I settle in with my novel.

A scraping noise jars me from my book. Something hitting the roof? A tree branch … no … footsteps?

Assuming that Michel has forgotten something, I return to the window. I scan the tree-lined street from our living room, but it looks quiet. I chalk it up to lack of sleep, yet I sense someone watching me.

The planter on the porch, though, has been overturned, and it's definitely annoying me. How long has it been that way? Without further thought, I leave the house with a broom to clean up the mess.

A man stands on the bottom step.

No, not a man—a vampire, clothed in a stylish tunic, dark trousers, and leather boots that stop at his knees.

I freeze, my palms sweating on the broom handle. Should I make a run for it? But I'll never make it inside before he reaches me. I have no weapons.

And my son is inside, alone.

Oh God, where are you, Michel?

We stand staring at one another. He's dazzling.

I fight to catch my breath. "Who are you?" I whisper, not sure if I'm breathing.

"My name is Victor." He smiles, coming up one step.

I think I push at him with the broom. "What do you want?"

"Please, you misconstrue my intentions. I don't mean to frighten you." He comes up another step, and I take a breath.

Why do I believe him? He's so powerful, I can feel it caressing my arms and legs. "I asked you, what do you want here?"

"Michel cannot protect you," he whispers, his voice raspy, yet sexy. "Not in the long run, anyway. Yes," he adds, maybe seeing surprise on my face, "I have met your beloved Michel. He came to the catacombs, looking for his best friend Christian."

"Christian?" I lean into the broom, no longer relying on it as a weapon.

"Yes, Christian Du Mauré. Michel told me all about him. Michel loves his friend very much, but he is useless to you. He will grow tired of his responsibilities to you and your son. Once that happens, you are both doomed, for what brought you together is your love for Christian, no? Eventually, he will grow frustrated and bored and leave you both.

"I know that you are a descendant of Josette Delacore, who seeks only to destroy you and your son. She is here in France, and it is only a matter of time before she finds you. When she does, she will tear you both into tiny pieces. No one will ever know you existed."

I struggle to breathe. Who is this vampire, who has clearly come here to deliver a message that expresses all of my unspoken fears? "Where is Christian?" I ask, forcing out each word. "Do you know where he is?"

"He is alive," the vampire says, "but that is all I can tell you. Is he the father of your son?"

"I don't know." I'm trying to gain control of my emotions, but I can't stop shaking.

Neither one of us speaks, though I have a million questions.

"Perhaps," Victor says, "when the time is right, we could meet alone. There is much to discuss. I will be in touch, Amanda. Watch yourself."

With that, he's gone.

Chapter 22
Michel

2011—Paris

Dared I say that I was becoming frustrated in my search for my friend? I finally decided I needed to go to the place I so dreaded, so I found a cabbie to take me into the forests outside of Paris.

Actually, I hypnotized him, which I hated to do, but it was necessary.

I had promised Amanda that I would search for Christian, and for the past year, I had avoided the one place I might have found him. Perhaps I was afraid of what might await me. Christian and I had been inseparable, and I had thought that nothing would ever come between us—that is, until he'd got it in his head that Josette Delacore was still alive and had left us.

I wasn't sure what I was hoping to discover in the remains of the Château des Singes. I relied on my eighteenth-century memory and a current map of France on my iPhone to guide me there. As I sat in the back of the cab, feeding directions to the driver, I closed my eyes and drifted back, to the last time I had visited this godforsaken château.

~

Her body was covered in bruises and bite marks.

Though hidden by her normal attire, once naked in the candlelight, her pale skin was dotted with them.

"Jo, what is this ...? ... Who ..." I was without words or an adequate way to ask her what had happened. I was only one of many of her lovers. Perhaps her husband Luc had done this ... and who was I to raise the issue? I had no claim to her.

At first, she tried to ignore me, pretending she did not hear me, but I scanned her dark eyes for an answer. I found none until she pulled me closer. Then her tears fell.

This was so unlike her. Was she with child again?

I pulled her close, cradling her trembling body with mine. "What is it, my love?"

"It's that fat cow, Henri Pilou. ... He's wicked, he—"

"You are sleeping with Henri Pilou?"

Between sobs, she explained how he kept giving her clothing, diamonds, pearls, and in exchange she let him basically do whatever he wished. All for the sake of wealth. I remained calm, but I knew what I had to do, for she would never, ever leave him.

He was a rich and powerful sadist who would never let her leave him.

I had to devise a plan to make sure he could never hurt her again ... but she could never know his fate.

* * *

The carriage whisked me out of Paris on a warm September night. We encountered only one other carriage while riding on the old road that cut west through the Bois de Boulogne into the Forêt de Rambouillet. The summer social season was over. As far as I knew, Christian was with Josette for the evening, which would give me the time I needed to end the reign of Henri the Terrible.

   The driver had been sufficiently hypnotized to follow my instructions, and I had no doubt that he would do so.

   I called for him to stop as we approached the dirt road. He would remain here until I summoned him later.

   My footsteps made no sound as I crept up the gravel driveway. I imagined that the servants were asleep. Light penetrated the darkness from a second-floor window—presumably their bedroom.

   Cricket song filled the night air. I moved around the right side of the house until I was facing the French doors that led into the library. A pane of glass fell into my hands when I tapped it with the hilt of my dagger and gave me just enough room to reach in and unlock the doors.

   The house was dark, but I had no trouble seeing as I made my way to the foyer and up the massive staircase.

   I heard someone snoring and headed towards the sound. I opened a door slowly, revealing a bed in which lay a lump on its side under a coverlet, beside a dying fire. White-blonde hair spread across her pillow. Madame Pilou. I watched her chest rise and fall, her snoring growing louder.

   I knelt down beside her bed and loosened her nightgown. Her pale flesh jiggled in the moonlight. Though she was less despicable than her husband, she had no right to live, either.

   I plunged my fangs into her fat neck. She startled awake, but too late. I wrestled her down, pinning her to the bed. She tried to kick me and missed. Soon, as I took every last drop of blood from her, her heart slowed.

   "What are you doing to my wife?"

   I released myself from her neck just as Henri Pilou charged toward me. "I remember you," he shouted. "You're—"

   I drew my dagger and jumped at him. My blade sliced into his chest, ripping a chasm from his neck down to his groin. Blood spurted through his hands as he tried to stop his entrails from slipping through his fat fingers.

"That," I snapped, "is for Josette."

Pilou fell, writhing onto his Aubusson carpet. I stood over him and watched as he slowly bled to death. He tried to scream, but there was only blood.

When it was over, I summoned the cab driver. We wrapped Pilou up in the carpet and carried him outside. I then lifted the fat cow, Madame Pilou, and carried her limp carcass out into the night. We loaded both of them into the carriage.

I instructed the driver to drive to Brittany and not stop until he reached the Atlantic Ocean, where he was to dump their remains.

I thought about burning the wretched château to the ground, but I settled for ransacking as much jewelry as I could load into my coat pockets.

On arriving home, I tossed my bloody clothes into the fireplace, took a hot bath, and secured the ruby rings, pearls, and chatelaines in a chest I kept hidden.

Call it financial security.

Chapter 23
Michel

I leaned forward to catch a glimpse of the château through the trees, a huge silhouette in the darkness. The cabbie made a right-hand turn onto the dirt road that would take us up to the château. A quarter moon lit the road, which glistened, coated by a first frost. I rolled down the window and sniffed the air. It was clean and crisp.

I had lined the pockets of my fur coat with my cell phone, my silver dagger, and a letter I had written for Christian. My plan was to leave it on the doorstep in the hopes that he would find it.

"Remain here," I whispered to the driver, stepping out of the back seat of the cab. "Turn off your engine." Then I made for the drive.

I held my breath as the main house came into view, constructed of brown limestone and flanked by two smaller wings, with a mansard roof and numerous windows.

Only then did I notice that a part of the roof of the left wing had collapsed in on itself. Most of the windows were broken. Trees and bushes encroached on the house as if at any moment the place would sink back into the forest. What a shame, what neglect!

I crept up to the front door, scanning the grounds behind me.

Peeking in the front door, I could see the once-sweeping marble staircase and the blue-and-white-tiled floor. The wrought iron railing was still in place.

God, Amanda would have loved this house, but there was no way I would ever bring her out here.

Then, out of the darkness nearby … *Crunch. Crunch. Crunch.*

Footsteps?

I turned, just as a familiar figure approached.

"We meet again," he said.

"Victor." I fondled the dagger in my coat pocket. Though I knew I could never beat him, I would not go down without a fight.

We stood staring at one another for … I don't know for how long.

Finally, I said, "I remember coming here when this house belonged to the Pilou family."

He nodded. "I hear it was quite the place to be at one time."

"Yes." I nodded, stepping back. "At one time."

"They mysteriously disappeared back in the eighteenth century," Victor said, studying the château.

"That's unfortunate." I would give him nothing.

Another long pause.

"You are looking for your friend, I assume." Victor came towards me. He also wore a long fur coat. I could have sworn he'd been raiding my closet.

"Just a hunch," I said.

"A hunch named Amanda Perretti, I presume?" He smiled.

That was when I realized that I had totally underestimated our presence in Paris.

He lifted his hand as if to stop me from making a fool of myself. "I went to your house in Le Marais. Actually, I have been watching you both for about a year now, since you came to me in the catacombs. Please," he added. "Don't worry. If I had wanted you dead, we would not be having this conversation."

"And I am supposed to take comfort in that, or be grateful?"

"Yes, you should, Michel, for you and your friend Christian have only remained alive through the good graces of a being such as myself—"

"Captain Andreas?" I should have known he'd had a hand in all this. "Oh, Christ."

"You know him as such, but I must share that we have been watching over you both for a very long time."

"Is Christian here?" I gestured toward the house.

"Yes, he is, but that is not why I am here. Don't worry, he is very much alive. However, his life should no longer concern you. You and I, though, have much to discuss."

With that, he sat down on the massive steps of the château and bid me sit next to him. What else could I do?

So I sat down, wrapping my fur around me. I stared into the darkness, still clutching the dagger in my right hand, hoping I would not need to use it.

He spoke into our silence. "I want Amanda."

His words cut through the cold air like fire. In fact, I could hear the passion and longing in his voice.

"Now," he said reasonably, "I could slaughter you right now, return to Paris, and take her and the boy, but I know how much you both mean to one another, so I have a thought."

"Okay," I muttered, unsure what else to say to him.

"I want to court her, with your permission—sort of like you are her father and I am asking for her hand in marriage."

I burst out laughing, unable to control myself. This was absurd.

"No, please don't laugh." He smiled. "I have thought this through. I have many houses at my disposal, any one of which I can use to set up her and the boy. I can protect her from all sorts of jealous, wicked vampires, such as Josette Delacore. And that way," he added, "you can remain in Paris and do whatever it is that you do."

"What happens when you tire of her? No offense, but trust me, I speak from my own experiences with mortal woman. We tend to love them until we don't and then we leave them to die … alone."

"No offense taken. I assume that you will be there to pick up the pieces if that happens, but she is truly magical, and I am besotted with her."

"You have met Christian?"

"Not officially, but I know he wants only the best for you both, and so this seems like the most civilized plan."

"And Josette?"

"She will give you no more trouble. You can count on that."

And with that, he stood up, so I rose, as well.

"And now what?" I asked, dusting off my coat.

"I will contact Amanda and begin … courting her. At the same time, you begin to detach from her. Believe me, she will allow me to protect her. Look," he said, "I know this is not easy for you."

I didn't know what to say. Did he expect a response? In truth, I was no more able to keep house than I was to fly to the moon.

Did I dare express relief?

No, I decided, that would be so shallow. And besides, perhaps he already knew all of that, as he seemed to know so many other things. I would play along and let him think he was controlling my fate as well as Amanda's.

"I love Amanda," I said finally, "but I want only what is best for her."

"I knew you were a realist above all else." He smiled and extended his hand for me to shake. "Now go, your cab is waiting."

But I hesitated, remembering. "I have a letter for Christian. If the time is ever right, would you see that he gets it?"

Victor nodded, and I handed it to him, though honestly, I doubted that Christian would ever receive it. Vampires were not that noble, despite all of their politesse.

As I walked back to the cab, I imagined Christian watching the entire exchange from somewhere inside the château. Did he know that Amanda and I were okay, that he had a son, and, most importantly, that we both missed him so much?

When I got to the cab, I glanced back at the house.

Was it my imagination, or was there a figure on the second floor, gazing out the window like a specter?

Chapter 24
Amanda

2012—Le Marais, Paris

I check my outfit at least three times before heading out. I think I look okay.

It's a balmy April evening, great weather for walking through Le Marais. I head east from our mansion towards the Pavillon de la Reign, a beautiful hotel in the middle of Place des Vosges. The incredible architecture, the bookshops and designer clothing shops along the way remind me of the West Village in New York City. I cross the Rue de Bearn and spot the eighteenth-century hotel.

I keep telling myself that my true hope is that this mysterious vampire, Victor, has information about Christian. However, since that night last fall when he appeared on our front porch, he's all I've thought about. I have to believe that and have faith that he will be honest … at least, that is what I tell myself.

I know, though, that it's a stretch. Vampires are generally self-absorbed and secretive, to say the least. Besides, why would he help us find Christian? There has to be something in it for him. The only question is, how willing am I to pay his asking price?

Michel has been encouraging me to go out lately— strange, but he does know how much I love art and museums. Friday night is my "date night" with the Louvre, which stays open until 10 p.m. I always promise to be gone no more than two hours and to be home in time for him to go out.

And besides, I received an invitation for tonight.

It read: *Meet me at the Pavillon de la Reine. Friday night. 8pm.*

Out of habit I always open the mailbox, though we rarely receive mail, and there it was this morning, a parchment envelope with no name on the front. I reached for it and was assailed by images.

Rocks and caves, dancing women, blood and a lust for mortal flesh.

A verdant field covered in mangled bodies.

A tribe somewhere mountainous and cold—Scotland, perhaps?

Versailles.

Loneliness.

Roman legions.

So much blood.

I recall his energy caressing me—power, lust, and age—but I didn't sense anything malevolent. He's old—much older than Christian and Michel—and he has an aura that is different, as if his maker was something much older and not quite vampire.

Then there's the fact that Victor's face changed, ever so slightly, when he heard Julien cry. I felt at once so vulnerable but still safe. He could have slaughtered the two of us, and yet he delivered a message, then was gone.

Maybe I'm crazy to be out here tonight.

The glass windows of the restaurant open onto the courtyard. As I approach the entrance, I search the crowds and spot the maître d', but before I can say a word, he gestures for me to follow him. I'm so distracted by the surroundings and the sense of history that I almost don't notice when he stops in front of a candlelit table with matching leather benches.

Victor stands to greet me, stunning in a green shirt tucked into high-waisted black trousers and knee-high, high-heeled boots, which make him tower over me. A silver hoop dangles from his left ear, and a tattoo of a circle with a dotted center is slightly visible through his sheer shirt. Did he raid Michel's closet? "Ah, mademoiselle, you do me quite the honor." He smiles and motions for me to sit.

My head is full of so many questions that it causes an adrenaline rush. I reach for the chair back for support. I have to be strong and show him I'm not afraid, though my palms are sweaty and my heart racing, which he will no doubt detect.

Really, it's no use pretending.

"Please, sit down," he says. "You have nothing to fear from me."

Hesitantly, I sit.

Victor directs the waiter to bring us the most expensive bottle of Champagne. Like Michel, Victor appears almost human, which probably comes from spending a lot of time around mortals. It shows in his hand movements, his social graces—a survival skill. Perhaps he's never owned a nightclub like Michel, but Victor likely spent a lot of time where mortals tended to congregate, and in the twenty-first century, that's in bars and nightclubs.

We sit staring at one another in silence. Where to begin? My natural inclination is to launch in with my questions, but I'll try to be silent and let him speak. Hard as it might be to do.

Eventually, the waiter brings us Champagne and two flutes. I wonder what a two-hundred-and-fifty-year-old bottle of Champagne will taste like. *A bottle as old as Christian and Michel.*

"Thank you for coming tonight," Victor says. "I realize this is a most unusual situation." He exudes charm.

Something stirs within me that I haven't felt for a very long time.

He reaches out and gently touches my hand. "May we drink a toast?"

"Okay ...?"

"To your future and mine." He downs his glass and licked his lips while I sit in amazement. How has he created the illusion of drinking something other than blood?

I take a sip. Honestly, I've never tasted Champagne so exquisite. I close my eyes and drink again. It's so dry, so smooth that I feel my entire body relax.

"Not bad, eh?" Victor leans forward, clinking glasses with me. "Sometimes old age is a good thing."

"It's … I'm not sure I have the words. I've never tasted anything quite like it."

"Most mortals have not. It's a rare Champagne from the court of Louis XVI."

I know from my research at the Met that the French court had its own label. "Do you always share such a rarity with a mortal woman you've just met?"

"One rarity with another, wouldn't you say? You possess much vampire blood, yet you still appear mortal. How is this so?"

I lean in to whisper. "How can a vampire drink Champagne—or anything, for that matter?"

"Just like you, I am much more than I appear to be."

He refills my glass, which I lift impulsively.

As the bubbles tickle my throat, I grow calmer—never mind that I have no idea who this vampire is, though he feel strangely familiar. Perhaps that's why I came in the first place.

Victor takes another sip. "How old is your son?"

I stiffen.

"Please, Amanda, relax," he says. "I am curious, that's all."

"He's fourteen months old."

"Where is his father?"

The question assumes he knows that Michel isn't Julien's father. And it's a reasonable assumption. I mean, how could a vampire father a child, right? I try to think of an answer that's honest yet won't leave me any more vulnerable than I already feel. "He's away … traveling on business."

He snorts so suddenly that Champagne squirts out of his nose.

I feel like I should say something. "It sounds far-fetched, I know."

"Do you think I'm that gullible?" He dabs his face with his napkin and gives me a warm smile, even for one of the undead.

"No, not really … I'm sorry. It was disrespectful." Clearly he knows I am not telling the truth. Though I should be afraid, his manner comforts me.

His necklace catches my eye. It's so unusual.

He watches me watching him.

"I was admiring your pendant," I say. "It looks Celtic. It's beautiful. Is it silver?"

"No, actually, it's iron."

He leans closer so I can study it. In the candlelight, it looks silver, but upon closer inspection, the piece has a different density, a weight to it.

"Would you like to touch it?" he says.

"No, thanks." I can't imagine confessing how I can see images, sometimes, when I touch an object.

He takes my hand. His energy pulses through my body, a strangely familiar feeling, like when Julien was born. My son's birth was not painful, but was instead a rush of hormones and emotions, unlike anything I ever felt before. There seems to be a strange connection between the two events—Julien's birth, and Victor's touch—but I can't make sense of it.

I turn my head just as he runs his cold lips from my hand to the inside of my wrist.

Something tightens in my groin, and I see stars.

Suddenly he's beside me on the leather seat. He turns my face towards him. I think I might faint. As he kisses me, the floor seems to fall out from under my feet.

I reach for him with such an intense longing that I scare myself, and sink into the seat, not the least embarrassed to be kissing someone so passionately in public. Then a gust of cool air envelops me, and an emptiness.

And I'm alone.

Voices buzz around me, glasses clink, couples eat their dinners, yet I'm not sure what to do, trying to make sense of what just happened.

Eventually, I stand up to leave. No one stops me, so I assume the Champagne has been paid for. I head outside into the bustling courtyard. I take a deep breath and head home. I can barely walk. I'm light-headed, as if his kiss dissolved years of grief.

What did he do to me?

My mind is clear for the first time in over a year, and when I stop on my front porch to take in the night air, I know that my life here in this house is a part of my past.

Chapter 25
Amanda

Fall 2012—Paris

Julien flashes his typical crooked smile, raising his arms to indicate that he wants to be picked up.

I smile, lifting him. He's heavier and more mature, though only twenty months old. His dark hair is wavy, and his once brown eyes are now a hazel-green. He no longer reminds me of Christian or Gaétan. He's my extraordinary boy, and no matter his parentage, I love him, beyond measure.

Julien most likely will never know his real father. Even more, how will I tell him one day that his father is, or was, a vampire, a creature so complex, so beautiful, and so tortured? How will I explain that I myself will barely age, as will his uncle Michel? Will Julien demand some sort of explanation for Michel's uncanny ability to read minds, his need for so little sleep, his acute hearing, and his love of darkness?

I know I'm getting ahead of myself, but there's so much to tell my son … yet what if by telling him I create more of a danger for him? Or would telling him protect him? He's a smart kid. One day, he'll ask questions about the people around him. I need to have answers ready.

I think back to the night when Victor came here with a message. *Michel cannot protect you.*

"Oh, doesn't this look yummy?" I ask, cutting up food on a small plate for Julien, who grabs a piece of chicken with his hands since he hasn't quite mastered silverware.

While he eats, I pour myself a glass of white wine, waiting for Michel to rise. When at last he appears in the kitchen, I kiss Julien good night and leave them alone to go upstairs to shower and change. Earlier today, I arranged for a cab to pick me up at 8 p.m., and suddenly I can't wait to walk the halls of the Louvre.

If I run into Victor … well, that'll be a bonus. Not once do I doubt that if he wants me, he'll find me there, easily.

I try not to dress too fancily. After all, I'm only going to a museum. I opt for my typical black ensemble: jeans, boots, and sweater. It's early April but the nights are still cool. I wear little makeup, figuring that I can spruce up once I get to the museum, and do little to my hair. I feel like a teenager again.

"*Bonsoir*, my dear." Michel kisses me on both cheeks. "You look ravishing."

I smile, knowing that he won't ask to accompany me. "And my chariot awaits. I'll be home by ten." I kiss Julien, who's covered in potatoes and carrots. Normally I never leave such a messy child, but tonight I need to get away. Michel will bathe him and put him to bed. "My phone is on, and I'll see you both later."

Usually, Michel says, "Remember, call—" but tonight he says nothing as I bolt towards the idling cab.

Once I confirm my destination with the driver, I sit back to marvel at the winding streets of the Marais. The Île Saint-Louis comes into view, awash in eighteenth-century splendor. Michel tried to secure an apartment there for us, but rents were too high. I try to imagine wandering the narrow streets on that tiny island in the Seine, named after Louis XIII and designed in the seventeenth century. Aristocrats lived there up until the French Revolution.

We turn in at the Rue de Rivoli. Cars and shops fly by. My cab driver curses every one of them in French. We approach the Louvre from the north side, the Richelieu galleries lit up in all their opulence.

After paying my fare, I enter the massive courtyard and head towards the Galerie du Carrousel, my pulse quickened. As always, the museum is beautifully lit, the stone illuminated in a golden hue. Anxiously, I pay my admission, turn left, and ride the escalators up to the ground floor. Straight ahead is the Court Puget, a cavernous room filled with eighteenth- and nineteenth-century French sculpture. I need no guide to take me through the sculptures, and I'm forever in awe of the ability of an artist to turn a block of marble into a three-dimensional work of art.

Rarely are the Napoleon III apartments open to the public, so I take advantage of the opportunity to go in and explore. Don't misunderstand—they're garish in the extreme, but I can't resist the sense of history in these rooms. Napoleon was to France like our George Washington in the United States, though Christian and Michel would argue that despite the art he brought to Paris, Napoleon destroyed the character of the original city.

The dining room is overwhelming. I stand behind the barricade, trying to take it all in, wondering what it must have been like to sit in this room surrounded by nobility, dignitaries from other countries, family and friends, and to dine in such splendor. I scan the room slowly, noting the massive length of the dining room table from one end to the other. Other museum patrons come up behind me, though we say nothing to one another. They stay briefly then move on. Meanwhile, I am rooted to the spot, trying to savor every moment, and it takes me a second to notice that I'm alone.

There's too much red velvet, but my eyes well up as I look in at the dining room with its two massive chandeliers, fifty dining room chairs, and more gold ormolu than anyone could ever imagine. I study the room in awe, and as I look down the length of the table, I see someone there.

Funny—I could have sworn the room was empty before.

But there really is someone sitting at the head of the table. Museums now use silent alarms, and I wait for guards to come rushing past me to apprehend the nut who thought he had the right to sit down in a museum display.

But no guards appear.

It's then that I realize who it is, sitting at the head of Napoleon's dinner table.

Victor smiles. I gasp. Slowly, he stands. His attire mirrors the room: silk trousers, a brocade frock coat, and fabric shoes with a slight heel, all in shades of red and gold.

I study his reflection in the mirror. His flowing auburn hair catches the light of the chandelier, and he looks, for a moment, like an angel.

"Ah, mademoiselle, we meet again." Casually, he unclasps the velvet rope and gestures for me to enter the dining room.

How can I refuse? As a museum professional, I am hesitant to jeopardize any of these historic artifacts, but my desire to be someplace forbidden overrides my professional sensibilities.

When he pulls out one of the massive dark wooden chairs and gestures for me to sit, I don't know what to say.

The chair is more comfortable than it appears. I keep waiting to be arrested, but still, no one comes.

Victor sits back down, reaches for the gold carafe and two glasses, which I assume are part of the table setting. He pours what appears to be white wine and hands one glass to me. It's quite an elegant and seductive gesture, and I take the glass graciously. I lean back, hoping for a vision to give me some of the history in the room, though no images come to me from the glass I hold.

He takes the other glass of wine in hand. "A toast to one of the most exciting periods in the history of any time, don't you think?"

The clinking of our glasses echoes through the room. I take a sip of the most incredible white wine I've ever tasted. It's cool and dry, and I savor it.

I glance to my left and catch his reflection again. He's beautiful. I feel like I've been transported back in time.

"You belong here, amongst these fine furnishings," he says, "as if you were born in the eighteenth century."

I smile. "When I worked in the Metropolitan Museum of Art, I was surrounded by antiquities, but nothing like this." I sigh. "How wonderful it must have been to sit here amongst men and women, nobles and the bourgeoisie, and engage in discourse. How freeing to talk and share writings and books among like-minded people."

He seems to be deep in thought. "Yes, this room is beautiful, but nothing like Versailles." He looks around and then slides closer to me. His eyes reflect the golden light from the chandeliers. "Napoleon was a bit heavy-handed on the velvet, wouldn't you say? Louis, on the other hand—"

"Which one?"

"*Quatorze*! Is there any other?"

At his vehemence, I'm almost afraid to dispute him.

"This is ... eh—" he shakes his head "—but Versailles. You have been to Versailles?"

"Yes, I've been there. It's breathtaking."

He takes my hand. "But you saw it from a twentieth-century perspective, as a museum, and not as it was: a residence."

"Yes, but I've done so much reading on Versailles," I counter. "I never thought about how many people lived there and how they would eat and drop their scraps in the hallways as well as—"

"The place stank." He shakes his head again. "It is not the sanitized world of today, or the diorama-like atmosphere of this place, but it was alive with beautiful young women in colorful silk gowns and white wigs piled high on their heads. So much ... excess ... court intrigue ... and yet it was stagnant with gossip and rumor. Then, when the young German queen arrived ... well, you know the rest."

It takes me a moment to figure out who he means by "the German queen." "You knew Marie Antoinette?"

"Let us just say that more than one vampire wandered the halls of Versailles and danced the night away in the Hall of Mirrors."

"Did you actually speak to her?"

"On more than one occasion. She was very young, yet smart and perceptive, and she knew all the sniveling aristocrats running around these rooms were against her, yet she held her head high and carried herself like the queen that she was. Even in the end."

I wonder about Christian. Though he never mentioned being at Versailles, I can't imagine he ever wanted to be a part of that world.

Michel, on the other hand …

"Do you think Christian or Michel were ever there?" I ask.

Victor shakes his head no, then hesitates. "But how can I be sure?" he says. "I would wander by from time to time, especially toward the end, sort of like your modern-day garbage man who cleans up the detritus of the fleeing aristocrats."

I'm feeling a little light-headed from the wine, but I'm mesmerized. I'm so lucky to be sitting here listening to him talk about my favorite period in history. I remember Christian telling me that they fled France in July of 1790, and though the city was in turmoil, Versailles remained untouched and unaware of what was coming.

"Yet you are not French," I say, though I'm unsure what makes me say it. I know so little about him. Still, although I sense that he isn't a Frenchman, he seems to have been seduced by and entrenched in French culture.

As he takes another sip of wine, I notice his iron pendant under his ruffled shirt, reflecting the light as if a beacon from another time and place.

"How old are you?" I whisper, not letting go of his cold hand.

"Let's just say that none of my tribal remains are here."

My mind whirls through information from my college European history classes. He's too light to be a Celt, despite his green eyes and red hair … not too tall, no intermarriage with the Vikings … but his pendant seems Celtic.

"I'll save you the guess work," he says, watching me. "The Romans called us the Caledonii, though I no longer remember the language I spoke or the life I lived as a child—"

"You are a Pict?" I can barely get the words out.

"Very impressive." He nods. "Once the Romans came, they built roads and a wall across our land. We had to fight to save our way of life, no matter the cost, but they were so many and, looking back, they were so sophisticated in their warfare.

"I was left to die on a battlefield and was offered eternity by one with whom I remain friends to this day. Back then, he was traveling under the guise of a Roman general, and so I fought beside him as a Roman, too. Then the legions abandoned Great Britain, returning to the Continent. Britain fell into the Dark Ages, and France faired a little better, so I guess you could say—yes, I never left France."

"Your maker … he is still—?"

"I cannot speak of him to you, at least not tonight. Perhaps another time." He smiles.

We stand. The room tips slightly, and I sort of fall into him.

"It's that really old French wine—that will do it every time." He laughs and pulls me toward him and gently kisses me. My body responds immediately, waves of desire passing through me like an electric current.

"Have you ever been to Napoleon's bedroom?" He smiles.

When I shake my head no, he gently guides me there.

Chapter 26
Amanda

Six months later, 2013—Paris

I'm not sure how to dress to visit La Maison des Rêves. Fall is barely holding on, and soon winter winds will whip through the streets of Paris. I have always hated winter. I associate the season with bleakness, death, endings and loneliness.

I've been really lonely in my own home. I've tried to deny it, but it's really bothering me.

Although the change is subtle at first, one night I realize that Michel and I have not spoken in weeks. I have no idea if he is even still coming home at night.

I get dressed—dark leggings, knee-high boots, and a long black sweater. I received an invitation in my mailbox to accompany Victor—or "V," as the note was signed—on a trip to La Maison des Rêves. A cab is picking me up at 7 p.m. sharp, and I no longer need to lie about my whereabouts, for Michel has made himself scarce.

I told Michel I was going to the Musée D'Orsay. He shrugged and, in his typical sarcastic tone, told me to "have fun."

It was funny at the time, but he no longer seems concerned about my welfare. I lived in fear of Josette Delacore for so long … actually, Michel and I braced ourselves for some sort of attack that never came. Was it more than just coincidence that around the time Victor came into my life, my fears vanished?

Andreas will do.

I pause, remembering the stranger again.

That was how Michel addressed him, as Andreas.

What do you do, show up every hundred years or so and steal more jewelry? Michel had asked.

I put on my Movado watch and silver hoop earrings, wondering who had stolen jewelry, and from where.

I'm not that little boy any longer. What do you want with us now? Michel had asked Andreas.

Who were Victor and this Andreas, really, and how were they connected to both Christian and Michel?

* * *

The cab meanders through the village square of a quaint medieval French town, turning right down a winding road with huge maple trees creating a canopy across the road.

"This is the place, mademoiselle," the cabbie says in broken English that I barely understand. He opens the cab door and nods for me to get out.

The moon is a white thumbnail cutting through the darkness.

Victor stands just apart from the shadows.

"Ah, mademoiselle." He opens his arms to embrace me. "I am so glad to see you. How was your journey?"

"Fine," I whisper as he hugs me. He feels warm and taut, and I try to remain calm and still. As he scans me, starting with my leather boots, I know he can feel my heart pounding. When our eyes meet, my heart flutters, and I have to fight to contain my excitement.

"Relax," he whispers, brushing a curl from my cheek.

I feel compelled to kiss him but hold myself back.

He speaks in perfect French to the cab driver, who drives away into the darkness.

How am I going to get back to Paris?

Before I can ask, Victor grabs my hand, and we turn onto a tree-lined gravel road, walking in silence with the company of the moon, which leaves slivers of light on the dark terrain. A slight breeze makes the air just crisp enough to be comfortable.

The road eventually cuts across a small, well-manicured lawn and leads up to a two-story, eighteenth-century stone house. It's stately, comfortable, with six sets of symmetrical windows on each floor, French front doors, and a mansard roof with a chimney on either end.

Once inside, the smells of wood smoke, candles, and fresh flowers assail me. The windows are open. I expected a dark, dank mansion with water dripping down the walls and mold growing in the darkest corners, rooms that had been closed up for too long, touched by loneliness and loss. Instead, we stand in a cozy foyer with glowing candles and fresh flowers on a circular table. The furniture that I can see is clean and polished.

Two hallways meet in the foyer.

We walked from room to room, each one more beautiful than the last, each filled with tasteful antiques. The dining room easily seats twenty people. A dark marble fireplace is the focal point of the living room, surrounded by sunken couches, large chairs, and beautiful tables. There's a library filled with books and a large desk.

"Victor, this is just beautiful." I sigh as we walk the entire first floor.

"Do you like it?" He smiles, coming closer.

"Who wouldn't?"

He stops. "Could you imagine yourself living here, with Julien?"

He must be joking, I think … but by now, I know better.

"I bought it from a valet in 1750," he says. "Actually, I killed him and seduced his wife. By the time she died at the ripe old age of thirty, she had signed it over to me."

I swallow hard at the images. "How many such properties do you own?"

"Five or so. I'm actually quite fond of this place, but if you like this house, it's yours."

My face must give me away.

He says, "It would be perfect for you and Julien."

"Victor … You're serious, aren't you? I don't know what to say. I mean, I have a beautiful house in Paris and a life with … That is, I'm indebted to Michel beyond words."

"And where is your Michel these days?"

Do I dare tell him that I'm not even sure Michel is still living with us? Am I setting myself up by giving anything away? Victor will know if I'm lying, though … and besides, I like him.

"Is he still your lover?" Victor asks abruptly.

I pause instead of answering, unable to adequately explain the status of my current relationship with Michel. In the silence, the air seems to shift, as if the temperature in the foyer has suddenly grown colder. I look up.

Victor's eyes have grown darker.

I step back. "I'm not sure. … Michel and I seem to inhabit the same house—that's all."

"This is only for you, Amanda. Only you and Julien." He turns around with outstretched arms.

"I would love to live here," I say slowly. "I love the privacy, and it's so beautiful … but would I be safe here?"

"No one would harm either of you here, trust me." He nods.

But how can I tell him that I'm loyal to Michel? … No, it's more than loyalty. We bonded in our shared grief, and I took comfort in being with him. How can I survive without him?

"Victor … I'm flattered, but…" I let the sentence end there.

"The offer stands, but only for you and your son. You must decide before we leave here tonight."

"Honestly, as much as I would love living here, I cannot manage it alone. And what would I tell Michel?"

"You leave Michel to me. Believe me, he will understand."

"Why are you doing this for Julien and me?" I ask, once we have walked the entire second floor and settled in the master bedroom. It all seems too perfect. Julien could have his own room. I could convert one of the smaller bedrooms into a playroom for him and another into an office for me. Each bedroom is completely furnished, with a four-poster bed, an armoire, and a writing desk. The antiques are authentic and stunning. It would be like living in my very own museum.

All I would need to bring would be our clothing.

Victor takes both of my hands in his. "You will be safe here, Amanda, trust me. Nothing can harm you."

"Josette Delacore will give it her best shot, Victor. She's a powerful vampire."

"I knew her when she was a kid doing parlor tricks with tarot cards. She is no match for us, and you have nothing to worry about, Amanda."

"Us?" I swallow. "Who is this 'us'?"

"The Ancient Ones," he whispers. "We have ruled the world of vampires for centuries now. Every vampire who now lives does so only because of us. We have total control."

"Then why has she been allowed to live all this time?"

"At the risk of insulting you, it was Christian's love for her that kept her from meeting a fate she deserved centuries ago."

"Then you have a connection to Christian you haven't told me about?"

"I am close friends with his father."

"You knew Phillippe?"

"No, I mean his true father, Ghislain, one of the Ancient Ones."

Chapter 27
Amanda

April 2014—La Maison des Rêves

Within the year, I'm living in a home I could have only dreamt of, along with Julien. I left Michel back in our town house, promising to visit with my son. When we parted, I cried and Julien wailed, but Michel appeared anxious for us to leave him, not even holding Julien one last time.

In time, I came to understand that Victor was not as benevolent a being as he made himself out to be, and although he was my lover and our protector, he has very little to do with our daily lives.

But when we first moved into the La Maison des Rêves, settling in took all my time and attention. I have more space than I'll ever use, but I feel more at home here than anywhere I ever lived once I left home.

Often I'm left alone during the day to read or write. I keep copious journals and study everything I can find about the paranormal, particularly vampires and witches. At night, I make a fire, have dinner, and wait for my lover to appear.

Sometimes I'm asleep when he silently approaches me, his form half in shadows, half visible in the firelight.

He's beautiful.

He must put a spell on us, for Julien never wakes to my screaming as my body shakes with each orgasm.

"Just a taste," he whispers, moving slowly inside me, bringing me closer and closer to what the French called *la petite mort*—the little death.

I turn my neck and wait for him to latch onto me. When he does, we both shatter as he drinks from me.

Darkness descends, and then I wake, alone in my huge bed, the fire dying as the sun rises.

I often wonder where he beds down, or whether he does at all, for he is an ancient being.

He smiles and brushes my hair from my face. "I cannot talk about the Ancient Ones."

Then he shares stories with me of the brazen and beautiful Violet, who dresses like a Goth warrior and loves to frequent the clubs just as he did. Her latest haunt is Berlin. There is the reticent Sébastian, forever the peacemaker. He was on the stones, ready for human sacrifice by the druid priests, when he was rescued by Boreas, another of the Ancient Ones.

When I ask about Ghislain, Victor grows unusually silent, as if by saying his name we might actually conjure him up. I learned that Ghislains' role was to keep law and order among their kind, though he had done two things that should have gotten him slaughtered by their king and queen: he slept with a mortal woman and begat a child—Christian— and he slaughtered his king and queen when they demanded that Christian, Michel, and I be brought to them. Thus by his actions, he all but disbanded the Ancient Ones, at least for the time being. He was Christian's true father, though Victor alluded to the fact that Ghislain was more than a vampire.

At any rate, Ghislain was noble, and I had him to thank for all of our long lives.

I did everything in my power to learn more than the basics about the mysterious being Ghislain, but Victor would not budge.

* * *

Of all the time we spend together, I think I like the winter nights best, when Julien and I finish dinner and lessons by the fire and then I put him to bed. Victor comes by later, and we sit by the fire in the living room and talk about as much of his long life as he'll divulge to me.

Though he won't let me tape-record him, I write everything down in my journals so I have a record of it all.

He promises to sneak me into Versailles, but what would we do with Julien? When he gets older, Victor says.

Still, Christian and Michel are always present, ever on my mind. I remind myself that I won't hear from Michel—that was the bargain we three struck, and Michel survived long before I was born and will continue to survive—but Christian seems like an ancient memory. Is he with Josette Delacore? If so, where?

Though I will always love Christian, he's fading from my memory. Josette Delacore is out there somewhere. Victor never mentions her name.

Once or twice, I brought up Christian, only to be assured that he was alive and safe, but that was all Victor would ever share with me.

As Julien gets older, we three take walks at night, or drive to some of the other properties that Victor owns. At some point, Julien began to call Victor "Daddy," and I kept reminding him that Victor was his uncle, not his daddy, but when Julien was about five years old, everything changed for us. He was old enough to begin to question our lifestyle, and the mysterious Victor began to show up less and less.

I found myself lying awake most nights, missing Michel. Where was he? How would he find us?

It would be years before I learned the role played by both the Ancient Ones and Victor in keeping Christian locked away. He'd manipulated both Michel and me for his own selfish gains.

* * *

Then, one March night on my birthday, Julien and I are playing cards after my favorite dinner of beef stew. As always, it's just the two of us. My plan is to devour a good book by the fire once I bathe Julien and put him to bed.

I'm just settled in the library when a knock at the front door startles me. We never, ever have visitors, and Victor has a key. "Who on earth—?"

I get up and peek out of one of the leaded glass front windows. A figure stands in the driving snow, wearing a floor-length fur coat with a hood.

Dressed like that, it can only be one person.

I throw open the front door with a happy cry and fall into the arms of the one vampire I knew would never desert me. I've missed Michel terribly for five years.

"Happy birthday, *mon ami*." He smiles, dropping his coat on a chair in the foyer.

I hardly have time to say his name before we're racing upstairs to my bedroom.

"How is Julien?" he whispers.

"Take a look for yourself." I open my son's bedroom door.

"God, he's grown up to be quite the man." Michel chuckles.

As I stand there, watching Julien curled up around one of his many stuffed animals, I realize that we three belong together.

I pray that Michel will decide to stay.

Chapter 28
Josette

2010—Paris

Often, I wandered the streets of Paris alone, marveling at how much it had changed over the centuries. Only the Latin and French Quarters and Le Marais were recognizable to me.

One night, purely by chance, I found myself on the Rue de Rivoli. Exhaust fumes, lights, and car horns assailed my senses, and too many pedestrians littered the streets, yet I tuned them out and found myself in a reverie, remembering the apartment I shared with my husband Luc Delacore. It faced the Passage Richelieu of the Louvre Museum, though then it was a foreboding palace, dimly lit and filled with many stray cats, perhaps to keep the rat population at bay. Michel had joked sometimes, pretending to stomp on the rats, and I would scream, and he would pick me up and carry me through the street until we were at my apartment, safe from the world of rats.

Always my protector, Michel. He could never bear to see me in pain.

Then the news about Monsieur and Madame Pilou and their mysterious disappearance had reached me. The salons had buzzed with rumors. What had happened to them? Their jewelry had been stolen, but their stable of horses and the cabinets of Sevres china were untouched. Had there been a scandal? Had they been murdered?

I had bided my time, but I'd known that Michel had had something to do with it.

He had seen my bruises.

Did I dare ask him? Would he tell me the truth?

When I'd brought it up, he'd brushed it off, unconcerned. "I don't know why you are so concerned,

Josette. The man was despicable. Maybe he and his cow of a wife decided to move to England."

"Michel, please, just tell me the truth. He meant nothing to me."

He'd risen from my bed and fumbled for his coat, reached inside and pulled out a small leather pouch.

Naked and glistening in the candlelight, he'd sat beside me. I'd laid back, equally naked, anticipating his touch.

Instead, he'd opened the pouch and sprinkled its contents—rings, bracelets, and brooches—across my breasts.

"Where did you get these?" Shocked, I sat up, scattering the gems onto the sheets.

"Are you not satisfied?" he whispered, pulling me towards him, kissing me roughly.

"With you, always."

He reached for a diamond ring and slipped it onto my index finger. It fit perfectly.

For a moment, I had thought he might propose, but instead he threw me back on to the sheets. As his cold kisses covered my body, all thoughts of the Pilous had vanished from my mind.

I'd never asked him about them again.

* * *

One night, after about a year of living in Paris, I returned home alone. Sarah had chosen to stay home, and Mathieu had yet to find any sign of the vampire he sought.

There was no word from Christian. I wondered if we would ever meet again.

As I turned the lock and stepped into the foyer, the sweet, pungent smell of fresh blood filled my senses.

My first thought was that Mathieu had found Amanda—it was not vampire blood.

"Mathieu," I whispered into the darkness.

When someone else stepped out of the shadows instead, I thought I would faint. "Ghislain," I whispered, feeling like that thirteen-year-old girl again in my mother's house. I clasped my hands in front of me to keep from shaking. I had disobeyed him by leaving Paris for California, and although I had known he would catch up with me at some point, I was ill-prepared.

The look on his face was one of possession, ownership, and pride, as if in beating me at my own game.

I tried to step forward, but my foot was stuck in something sticky.

Human blood, congealing.

I staggered.

"What are you doing skulking around the mortal girl, Josette?" he said. He had something in his hand. "I told you to stay away from them, but you continually choose to disobey me to further your own ambitions."

As he came closer, I saw what he held in his right hand. It could not be, and yet it was—Sarah's severed head. I gagged and choked back a sob at the sight of those electric blue eyes, staring vacantly. I hoped her death had been quick.

"You'll find the rest in the kitchen." He tossed the head at me by the hair.

I screamed as it rolled past, the gaping wound in her neck leaving a bloody trail on the Oriental carpet, but I did not need to ask why he had slaughtered her. At my command, she had befriended Amanda.

Had I been so stupid as to think he would not find out what I planned to do to her and her son?

I was afraid to utter a word, for despite our past centuries together, I still felt that I only existed at his whim.

"I made you a vampire," he said quietly, "which is all you said that you wished for, and although that should have made you happy, it has not. You still carry the grudge of your perceived abandonment by both Christian and Michel, and yet, for centuries, you professed your undying love for them both to anyone who would listen. You had your chance with Michel in London once, but now you will have another chance to be with Christian again."

He went on and on, about a new order, and the Château des Singes being rebuilt to its former glory, and I being the queen and Christian the king of vampires. It sounded crazy, but I dared not protest. He had not been holding *my* head.

"I am losing patience, Josette," he added. "I will refrain from telling him that you tried to murder Amanda. Otherwise, your head may roll, too. A carriage will be here at sunset tomorrow. Be ready to leave this city and never look back. Am I clear?"

I nodded, trying not to focus on Sarah's bloodied head laying at my feet.

He gestured towards the kitchen door. "Perhaps cleaning up the scraps of your human servant will remind you that we all serve a greater purpose."

* * *

When we arrived at the Château des Singes, I was both intrigued and horrified—two states of mind in which I generally found myself these days. Mathieu had been quiet beside me. Clearly, he had not wanted to leave Paris, but we'd had no choice. Sarah was dead, and I was about to embark on yet another journey, though I was not sure how much control I could exert with Ghislain present.

We were led into the massive foyer. God, how I remembered the parties here, hosted by the Pilous. I could almost smell the food and the wine and the blood. Beside me, Mathieu tensed up as well.

I felt him before I saw him at the top of the stairs.

Christian stood, radiant in gold knickers and a frock coat right out of the eighteenth century. He smiled at me, something he'd rarely done. Then his eyes moved to Mathieu. He flowed down the marble staircase. He took me in his arms rather stiffly to kiss me on each cheek. "Welcome, Josette."

Clearly, Mathieu was the prize he sought, for Christian quickly embraced my son. "Mathieu, it is so good to see you." His voice was soft and warm.

Ghislain stood watching us all from the landing. Did he approve?

The irony of the three of us being together was not lost on me. The family Christian had always wanted, but which had forever eluded him, now stood before him.

In a flash, I realized that I was beyond this charade, but I had no choice.

A valet gestured for us to follow him upstairs and as I ascended the staircase, memories of being here with Michel assailed me.

The sky-blue hallways, the images of monkeys on the walls, the shiny black-and-white tile floors.

As I passed the doorway to the room that had once been mine, I saw the mortal girl I'd been, entwined among so many vampires, thinking herself invincible and all knowing.

How stupid she—*I*—had been.

Chapter 29
Christian

Ten years later, 2020—Château des Singes
Le Bal Masqué ~ Halloween

"How do I look?" Josette beamed up at me, twirling around like a child. She had always loved parties, and our annual masked ball was no exception. When she and Mathieu had first arrived here, ten years ago, Ghislain had thought that a masked ball would be the most appropriate way to ingratiate ourselves into the present ranks of the Parisian vampires, and so we'd begun hosting one.

The tradition, begun by aristocrats centuries ago, stemmed all the way back to my youth. The idea was that the aristocrats could frolic and fornicate with whomever they chose as long as everyone was wearing a mask. Had it been sheer boredom that made them act the way they had?

I'd never understood frivolity and games. Even when I was mortal, I'd hated parties.

Now, I had to admit that there was something prurient and forbidden about the atmosphere once you covered your face. The rules of polite society no longer applied. I always wore a wig, for my flowing blond hair would have given me away, though I tended to wear the same costume year after year.

Josette and I were trapped here, and only in the last year had my father taken to leaving us alone to manage our pathetic lives. Still, we were bound by wards that even Josette could not decipher, and God knows how she tried.

Speaking for myself, initially, time passed incredibly slowly. I was given anything I asked, except permission to go outdoors.

When I had first arrived here, Ghislain had done everything possible to engage me, but it hadn't worked. I had missed my best friend, and Amanda. How could I have been so stupid as to leave them and return to France?

I had tried journal writing, but that had made me feel even more morose and sorry for myself. Instead, I'd traded the pen and journal for paper and charcoal, and soon, I'd found myself drafting a layout for the library and the ballroom. More charcoal and paper had appeared. Ghislain had seemed not to want to be seen, so he'd left a massive amount of paper and charcoal in one of the bedrooms I had taken to using because of all the windows, which let in much sunlight.

After her arrival, Josette would sit and watch me create. Sometimes we'd both laugh at my ideas. Though I had to admit that I loved the sound of her laugher, I frequently drifted back to New York and my life there. Amanda and my son filled my thoughts, and blood tears would flow. How could I have left them? If only I had thought through my actions, and not simply acted on impulse, then the three of us would still be there together, and I would have a son and some semblance of a family life.

I could not even blame Josette, for she was a pawn, too.

One day, I had asked for oil paints and canvas, and suddenly, it was as though I'd been transported back to my studio on the Rue de Rivoli with Michel and Étienne, a young boy we had found wandering the streets of Paris, who had eventually become our human servant.

We had been such young vampires then. I'd thought the world simple and easy to control. Josette had been just a girl, and I'd thought she would be mine forever, but those three years had passed quickly, and I had lived centuries of regret over them ever since.

I painted Amanda as I remembered her, sitting in our library by the fire, serious and with a book in hand, thinking herself so wise. Josette hated these paintings, but there was nothing she could do.

When I painted Michel, I captured him as I remembered him in our youth, not as the vampire he'd become.

I had Josette sit for me as she had done as a young mortal. I reminded her of the time I had painted her on the Pont Neuf while Michel stood guard over her, for once the sun set, the bridge was a dangerous place for mortals. There had been nights in which Michel and I had hunted mortals there, too, and I tried to capture those places.

Over time, I created quite a few canvases. When I looked at them, scattered around my "studio," I felt a sense of satisfaction I had not known in a long time.

Josette suggested jokingly that perhaps I could sell the paintings and become both rich and famous, two things she knew I abhorred. Who needed fame when you had immortality, and money? I had more than I knew what to do with. A lot of good it had done me.

Ghislain sometimes hovered in the doorway, a towering, brooding figure. Were we some sort of science experiment to him? Other times, another vampire accompanied him, shorter, with auburn hair and green eyes. He seemed to pay particular attention to me, and I could have sworn he did not like me, though I could never figure out why. Mostly, though, Ghislain left us alone.

Meanwhile, I would find myself lost in my painting.

Then, one day, I realized that, by my actions, I had accepted my father's offer to live here and make a go of ruling the vampire world.

Not that I'd had a choice.

Perhaps he had not trusted us initially, and that was why he had hovered over us while my queen and I settled into a daily routine.

Though I rarely saw Mathieu, Ghislain seemed more closely connect to him. There was something about Mathieu that frightened me. Was it his dark, soulless eyes, or his lingering in the shadows? I knew he had died at the hand of my maker Gabrielle, whom Josette and I often fantasized about slaughtering, but as far as any of us knew, she had left Paris.

* * *

"Maybe tonight is the night?" Josette's face glowed. She asked this same question every year at our masked ball, hoping that Gabrielle would be among the guests.

Although we had spoken of the possibility many times, and had even gloated over it, only if Gabrielle were present at our annual ball could we execute the heinous plan Josette and I had made. Ghislain had promised us both that we would have the honor of ending Gabrielle's immortal life, for I had been betrayed by her when she had attempted to murder Josette and had succeeded in killing Mathieu.

We'd designed, and Ghislain had had built, a *petit trianon* of our own, if you will—a small palace, a respite away from prying eyes … only it was, in fact, a marble death trap. The only trick would be to get Gabrielle inside it.

In our less sane moments, Josette and I had conspired to capture my father and lock him away, as well, so that we could be free of him, but that would have been impossible, for he was neither of this earth nor really one of the undead. Nothing could contain him, nor could fire destroy him.

Many a night as we lay together in the darkness, I spoke of a day that I might choose to die, to no longer live as a prisoner in my eternal body.

"You can't be serious," she whispered in my ear, spooning me, her cold, tiny body pressed tightly against me. "After everything we have been through? You cannot leave me, Christian."

She knew me better than that, and because she did, she knew that I was, indeed, serious. One day, I trusted that I would know when all of it needed to end for me, and now that we were free to roam the grounds, could immolate myself on any given day.

How we danced that night. I wasn't not sure why, but I was actually happy, as I scanned the room for the two vampires who would bring me even more happiness: Gabrielle, so I could finally end her miserable life, or Michel.

How I missed my friend. I would have known him anywhere, had I but seen him. Year after year, I had wandered the crowds looking for him. He'd never come. I realized that I had no idea where he might be living. I assumed it was Paris, but who really knew? Perhaps he and Amanda had gone back to New York.

With my tendency to grow bored rather quickly, I positioned myself on the dais overlooking the crowd and sat back to watch.

Hours later, Josette sat beside me, and when she leaned over to whisper in my ear, I knew what was coming. "I think she's here, Christian."

I scanned the room, past the beautiful, silk-clad and powdered-wigged dancers and colorful masks, but did not feel a thing. We were connected by blood, and I had always believed we could sense one another's presence … but perhaps not.

"She was heading towards our *petit trianon* with a younger vampire." Josette smiled.

"Let them settle there." I was good at waiting.

We always left the three sets of French doors in our *petit trianon* open, to encourage guests to wander in and out freely, and in the hope that one day Gabrielle might find her way inside and do exactly what Josette was telling me had finally happened.

Josette pulled on my sleeve until, at last, I let her lead the way through the ballroom, out the French doors, and down the torch-lit stone path towards our very own death trap.

Through the swaying sheer curtains, I counted more than one vampire moving about the dimly lit room, which was resplendent with silk couches and torchieres. The marble walls glistened by the light of the chandelier that burned brightly overhead. Each step I took felt like a lifetime, and I still could not believe it was really happening.

Our plan was simple—seal the doors and release the chandelier, for no true vampire could escape fire.

Josette crept away from me, towards the farthest of the three sets of French doors. We had practiced over and over, talking through our plan. I would quickly close the doors on the right, and, she, the doors on the left, and then the two of us would latch the center set of doors. The switch to drop the chandelier was right there on the outside wall. It was a simple plan if we moved quickly enough and remained undetected.

A tangle of flesh caught my eye. Gabrielle was riding a mortal, caressing him as she drank his blood.

For a moment, I flashed back to my own youth, and turning my neck to her in my barn on a March night in 1757. I'd been twenty years old, and so naïve. How many more young men had she turned, used, and murdered, just as she had done to Mathieu? I wanted to slowly rip her to pieces. Even fire suddenly seemed like too easy a death for her.

On another divan, a vampire held down a mortal girl, her face masked, but her wig on the floor beside them. He was, for lack of a better word, raping her.

I crept to my position. Focusing on Gabrielle, I slowly shut and locked the first set of French doors. I didn't look at Josette, but I knew she was doing the same. We had worked and planned and fantasized for too long for this very moment to ruin it, and it was perfect. They had not noticed.

Meanwhile, I stood transfixed, watching my nemesis. Centuries fell away, and it was as though I were a boy again. How different my life would have been if she had never come along.

Out of the corner of my eye, I noticed Josette at the middle set of doors. Quickly, she latched them just as someone else emerged from the shadows inside our death trap: my son Mathieu. He had spotted Gabrielle and was striding towards her.

Dear God ...

As if in slow motion, Josette unlatched the doors again and ran towards him, her face a mask of horror.

Gabrielle turned to see both Mathieu and then Josette coming at her.

In less than a moment, Mathieu was upon Gabrielle, ripping at her clothing, trying to subdue her, but she was a much older vampire.

Josette lunged at him, trying to drag him away, screaming at him to get out, but he was frenzied, striking Gabrielle, trying to pull her neck towards him.

In one quick motion, Gabrielle lashed out. Something silver flashed in the candlelight. Mathieu grabbed his throat.

Anger flooded me, yet I could not move.

Mathieu dropped with Josette wrapped around him, trying to protect him from further harm.

It was too late. My son's head lolled. Gabrielle had nearly beheaded him, killing him once again.

Finding the strength to move, I ripped off my mask and the stupid wig and ran towards the flames. Someone yanked me back with such force that I landed on my back on the lawn. Victor and my father stood over me, having pulled me away as if I were a child.

Curled up in a ball, I watched in horror as my father locked the middle set of doors and threw the switch to lower the chandelier, then closed my eyes against the terrible screams from within, unable to watch the inferno that engulfed my past, my present, and my future.

The heat threatened to incinerate even me until Ghislain pulled me farther away, dragging me by my arms. He said something to Victor in a language I did not recognize, though I thought I heard the name Amanda. What did he have planned for her?

Still I couldn't move.

Through the smoke and smells of death, I watched my world curl up into the night sky, a sky full of stars and so much promise.

A long time later, Ghislain picked me up like a child and threw me over his shoulder.

After that, there was only dread and darkness.

PART THREE
She burned too bright for this world.

Chapter 30
Julien

2030—La Maison des Rêves

I buried my mother two days ago.

Amanda Perretti was a young forty-eight years old, and as I look around the only place I have ever called home, I feel lost without her.

I'm twenty years old. The entire world is ahead of me … yet all I feel is numb.

Villepreux is a small town about two hours southwest of Paris. My mother and I moved here when I was two years old, and though I don't remember much until my fourth birthday, what I do remember is feeling safe in this rustic country house we called home. The scents of wood smoke, hearty stews, candle wax, and old books were as common to me as the stories my mother shared about the house. Built in 1710, our house had wide-planked floors and working fireplaces. The furnishings were all original, dating from the eighteenth century. We lived in a time capsule. It even had a name: La Maison des Rêves, the house of dreams.

I can't remember a time it wasn't the two of us.

My friends rarely came here. Not that I couldn't bring them over, but my mother preferred to be alone, though she never came out and said as much.

As I grew up, we spoke of everything: American history, for she was from New York, and European history, art, and museums, for she had worked in the Metropolitan Museum of Art when she was a young woman.

Our house was filled with books, for my mother devoured books like other people might consume a good meal. Paintings, hundreds of years old, adorned the stucco walls of our living and dining rooms. They were beautiful, all originals.

Don't ask me the names of the artists.
* * *

The sun is sinking into the shadows of an early
autumn evening. I find myself staring out the kitchen
window, past the back lawn, into the woods. There used to
be flower gardens in the spring and summer months, cradled
by the beautiful woods that surround our house.

As a child, I remember, I was afraid of the woods.
My mother only allowed me to play there during the day.
Like a green curtain, the trees shielded us from outsiders. I
don't ever remember hearing a car drive past or an airplane
fly by high overhead. It was as though we existed apart from
the modern world.

Sometimes, she slipped out at night when she thought
I was asleep, when really I was curled under the covers with
a good book and a flashlight. When I asked her where she
went, she explained that a walk in the woods helped clear her
head and not to worry. But how could I not worry? She
forbade me to go to the woods at night, so why did she
venture there herself?

One night, when I was twelve, a nightmare woke me.
I went automatically to find her. I always took comfort in
knowing that she was just down the hall, usually reading in
bed, but that night, when I went to her bedroom—complete
with a large four-poster bed, bookcases and comfortable
chairs, and always a fire in the fireplace—I found it empty. I
knew where she had gone, and so I followed her to the
woods, despite her warnings—just a boy who wanted to
protect his beautiful mother.

The moon was already high in the sky, a white orb
tossing patches of light onto the dirt path to guide my way. A
warm breeze stirred the treetops. The woods looked and felt
different that night. Maybe it was the full moon, but the air
felt charged, and yet I wasn't afraid. The smell of fresh earth
was heady.

I heard a strange sound. It was subtle at first, but as I got closer, I could only have described it as a low-pitched moan. I tried to imagine what sort of animal could make such an eerie yet passionate sound. I had never heard anything like it.

Through the trees, white shapes moved in the grass within a stone-encircled clearing. I stepped towards them: naked bodies tangled up in one another, moving as one. I knew my mother's voice; she sounded like she was moaning, almost crying. Another dark-haired woman with limbs that seemed to glow in the moonlight lay over her, their arms entwined. What was she doing naked in the woods?

The woman was kissing my mother, and I inched closer, my curiosity getting the better of my embarrassment over spying on her. My mother had always been such a mystery to me, and here she was, like a goddess, tangled with another woman in the darkness. Perhaps that was why they met in the woods rather than risk me finding out about them.

I looked more closely at the other figure, which shifted enough for me to realize my mistake. It was not a woman but, in fact, a man, tall and thin, with dark curls that fell around his shoulders and a porcelain-like body, like a Greek statue.

I knew I should back away and leave them alone. This was nothing a boy should witness his mother doing, but I was transfixed.

My mother held the stranger, kissing his hair and moaning "Michel"—his name?—over and over. He was not hurting her but giving her pleasure. It was pleasure I heard in her voice.

He pulled away, and something dark ran down my mother's neck.

Was that her blood?

Was he a vampire sucking her blood? Was that why she'd forbidden me to go into the woods at night?

I wanted to rescue her, but I feared being caught. I turned back and ran to the house, not looking back.

Afterward, I never mentioned it to her, though the image of the two of them stayed with me always, never far from my waking thoughts.

* * *

I've been studying journalism at the Sorbonne, far enough away from home to feel independent but close enough to hop a train back. It was four o'clock in the morning when I received the phone call. The train ride I took from Neuilly-Sue-Seine was a blur.

According to the police, my mother's body had been found in the decaying grass and leaves in the woods behind our home, four days ago. I was told by the neighbors that it looked as if she had lain down to take a nap. There were no visible signs of a struggle, no gunshot wounds or knife marks, no bruises or cuts. Nothing visible to indicate how she had died. She had neither friends nor enemies that I knew of. How had it happened?

As I stand here, in the empty kitchen, my thoughts awhirl, the "night in the clearing," as I came to call it, comes to mind. I wander out of the kitchen, into the library, struggling with that memory. If I had stopped her that night, would she still be alive?

If a house has a center, a core, this room, this library, is it—small but with large windows that open onto the back yard. Shelves and shelves of books line the walls. A large desk and two chairs center the room.

She did all of her writing here—she was a prolific journal writer who never shared with me where she kept them, and only ever joked about what to do with them when she passed on. "Burn them." She'd laugh, pointing out back. "Make a huge bonfire out of them."

Now she really is gone, and what am I supposed to do? Did she really want me to destroy years of her history in this house?

One of our distant neighbors, who was out walking his dog in the woods, found her and called the police. A lawyer by profession, he has been very helpful navigating French inheritance laws. My mother had no last will and testament. There was no paperwork declaring her the owner of our house, but according to French law, she owned it by the very fact that she lived here for eighteen years. He also made all of her funeral arrangements, for I was all but useless.

I assume the house will be mine, just as all her worldly possessions are now mine as well.

I left the Sorbonne in a hurry, with barely time to send an email to one of my professors, explaining my sudden leave of absence. As I look around at the house that cocooned the two of us, I wonder if I will return to school this semester at all.

What will happen to our home? I love this house and have no plans to sell it, but who would take care of it if I return to classes? It's times like these that I wish I knew who my father was—or at least knew his name. Although my mother and I talked about everything, there was one topic that we never spoke of: him.

I never pressed her for answers about her past. It was a forbidden subject, a place she rarely shared with me. But I never knew for sure why discussion about my father was off-limits. I never got the sense that it was out of anger. I knew almost nothing about him, except that he was French, very handsome, a loner, and—oh, yes, she once mentioned that he was tall and that he loved to read.

That narrowed it down to at least ten million Frenchmen.

I imagined the two of them reading for hours and hours amidst piles of books, never taking their eyes off the written word except to gaze at one another.

One summer night, when I was young, I sat on my king-sized bed and wrote a list of everything I knew about my father. To this day, it barely fills one notebook page. He was, and is, an enigma.

I never even saw a photograph of him. In fact, there was not one photograph of any of us in the house. There are plenty of oil paintings, including one, particularly beautiful, of my mother, which hangs here, in the library. She mentioned that she sat for the portrait when she was only in her twenties, but it seems to me that she had not aged.

If her past was a closed book, it was truly a very bizarre novel, and one to which I was never privy.

She was beautiful, both petite and commanding, with dark curly hair and light green eyes. I watched the way men stared at her, though I wondered why she never dated or married. Perhaps she found peace here alone, but as I got older, I saw her differently.

Who or what had she hidden from here in the woods?

Chapter 31
Julien

I spend a few days wandering aimlessly around our house, looking for—what, I'm not sure. Just as my mother's life was a mystery to me, it seems fitting now that her death is, too.

How ironic that our two-story house has six bedrooms, but no one ever stayed overnight. In fact, we rarely had guests. Our kitchen held a table large enough to seat twenty yet never sat more than the two of us. A rustic walk-in fireplace and French doors led out to our back yard, but we never held parties or entertained. Our dining room and two parlors were simply repositories for books and beautiful pieces of period furniture in tan wood and rich fabrics.

In a frantic attempt to locate any of her journals, I have searched every drawer and closet in the entire house but found nothing out of the ordinary—that is, until I try the closet in the library.

At first the door sticks. Did she not use it very often? I take a good look and notice the ornate golden lock.

Of course she kept her journals locked away. I never thought much of it. Clearly, she did not want her son prying into her personal life, though, as far as I could tell, she had no personal life. Yes, she had an active imagination, and she was very creative, but why such secrecy?

And where would she have kept the key?

Although she had little jewelry, the pieces she did have were antiques, and extremely valuable, as she had told me on more than one occasion. I never saw her wear any of it, but she described it as if it all belonged in a museum collection. She spoke of Marie Antoinette as though they were friends.

I thought she was joking at the time, but come to think of it, my mother rarely joked about much of anything. It was like she was living amongst bygone splendor, or had been designated a keeper of the past. But for whom?

I go upstairs, into her bedroom, and look through her only purse, then her massive armoire and the drawers in the dresser.

Nothing.

I check all the knickknacks on the fireplace and realize I have many more bedrooms to explore.

My search, however, yields nothing.

In her bathroom, half-burnt candles along with shampoos, a women's razor, and bath gels litter the window ledge near her claw-footed bathtub. I even check the medicine cabinet and the linen closet and a recessed area that holds a dresser and more shelves. I navigate tiny Limoges figurines, perfume bottles, and two old books, one stacked upon another.

Odd. My mother would never have brought books into a bathroom where they could have been exposed to possible water damage and dampness.

Hoping to catch the title, I catch my breath when instead both books turn in my hand as one. It is, in fact, a box made to look like a stack of books. I open the lid. Nothing inside except a Post-it note. Written in block letters on it are a single line: *Check the fridge.*

It makes no sense to me, and yet everything she did was deliberate, calculated and planned, so I do what she asked and jog downstairs to the kitchen.

The stainless steel refrigerator still seems so out of place in a kitchen with a stone floor, exposed wooden beams, hanging copper pots and dried herbs. The stove is cast iron and huge, and our colorful clay dishes sit behind glass doors in blond wooden cupboards. In the wintertime, we had all our dinners down here, sitting at the huge farmer's table with a roaring fire.

It was magical then, and so cozy.

I open the refrigerator, loaded with ceramic crockery full of leftovers from the reception I held here after her funeral. The neighbors brought so much food that I have meals for another week. I see nothing out of the ordinary, then think to open the freezer.

There sits a rather large Tupperware container. I didn't think that my mother owned Tupperware, much less knew what it was.

There is definitely something inside it, some sort of scarf or a piece of material. I take it upstairs so I can sit near the fireplace in the library.

Inside the Tupperware, wrapped in one of her silk scarves, I find several old photographs and a leather-bound diary.

The first photograph is definitely her with a boy I assume was her brother Ryan, another mysterious figure in her life. Even at ten years old, my mother looked so serious. I flip the picture over. In my mother's neat handwriting, it says *1992, Manhattan*.

The second photo shows the street sign for East 83rd Street, with a row of beautiful town houses. Perhaps she lived there, in Manhattan. The street looks elegant, and I wish she had taken me there. The back of the photo reads *#9*.

The last photo is dark and rather blurry. I carry it over to the table lamp to get a better look.

It takes a minute to make out the images of two long-haired women, standing together in front of a dark marble fireplace. One is blond and the other brunette. For a moment I think that one of them is my mother, but actually, the figures are men, not women at all.

The smiling dark- haired one on the right has his arm around the shoulder of the tall blond, who appears to be pulling away, a grimace on his porcelain features. Are they fashion models? Both men are certainly tall enough and handsome, with piercing eyes and strange clothes. The blond wears velvet trousers and a lacy shirt, like something out of the 1960s. His hair falls to his waist. The other model is entirely in black leather with lots of silver jewelry and hair so dark it's hard to tell where it ends and his shirt begins. He is exotic and beautiful.

My stomach knots.

I am sweating.

Oh my God, the man with dark hair—he was the one with my mother in the woods. My memory of that night in the clearing suddenly becomes tangible and real enough that I relive the feelings all over again.

I flip the photo over. *Christian & Michel, Manhattan, 2007.*

I set the photo down on the coffee table, pour myself a small Cognac, and sit down with the journal. It's cold in my hands, and I immediately recognize my mother's neat, small handwriting.

The journal falls open to an early entry dated 2011, in Venice Beach, California.

She would have been twenty-nine at the time, making me a one-year-old boy.

I turn the page and begin her journey.

Chapter 32
From the Diary of Amanda Perretti

Venice Beach, 2011

There was a brief time when Christian and I were together, and before that, I was searching for him: the man who saved my life one night in Central Park on the Fourth of July. If you do the math, I have spent more time searching for him than we spent together. How's that for a lopsided relationship?

I still find it painful to recall the summer night when my brother Ryan called, begging to meet. Like the fool I always was when it came to my brother, I went to meet him in Central Park, thinking that this time it would be different, that I could change him.

He tried to tell me he was hanging out in a club in the East Village, making money doing things he could only confess to in a mumble. He looked so old for someone so young, but that is what drug addiction will do. He was so thin, dirty-haired with bruised, paper-thin skin. All I wanted to do was take him home, clean him up, and show him another life.

But it was not to be.

Instead I watched him die, murdered by a monster who drank his blood right in front of my eyes and left his battered remains laying in the tunnel, and then came for me.

It's like a movie, one I replay over and over again in my head.

One moment the monster was coming for me.

The next, he too crumpled, his body igniting in a ball of flames as his severed head flew like a Frisbee through the air, cut off by a man wielding a machete.

The man was my savior, a two-hundred-year-old vampire, born in eighteenth-century France, now living in Manhattan. I would learn much more about him later, but upon waking in the hospital and recounting what I had witnessed, I felt like a crazy person, told by doctors and law enforcement that trauma had rendered me temporarily insane.

My brother's murder went unsolved.

I searched everywhere for the tall stranger with the flowing blond hair. I wanted to thank him, and perhaps, in finding him, I would know I had not been hallucinating that night in the park. That what I had witnessed was real. He might be able to answer my myriad questions.

Six months later, I found him quite by accident, and, despite his protestations, I continued to seek him out. He was a beautiful, enigmatic loner, lost in the modern world, held captive by his memories of a mortal lover he had left to the embrace of guillotine in Paris during the French Revolution. His name was Christian Du Mauré, and her name, Josette Delacore.

My meeting Christian took place more than a year ago.

I am the mother of a one-year-old son. My son and I have been sharing a cottage here in Venice Beach with Michel Baptiste, another vampire and the best friend of my savior Christian. Michel and I fled New York City and came here. Christian left for Paris, but we have lost all trace of him.

In dreams and visions, I see him in a decrepit mansion, surrounded by vampires who grovel at his feet, though I know not why. I would like to believe that he is waiting for the right moment to come back to us. Michel is more realistic, something I would never have guessed in watching him with women in the bar. Is Christian lost to us both? I cannot give up hope that he knows where we are, and so we patiently wait for his return.

I am alone in this world except for my son Julien and Michel.

I have to believe that Christian and I met for a reason. Not a day has passed that I don't think about Central Park and how I walked into a world that I never imagined could be real. It's more than falling in love and being thrust into the world of vampires. Doesn't love change you beyond recognition, leave you with a longing never to be truly fulfilled?

I look into my son's eyes, and I tell myself I should find peace and contentment there, but I am so afraid. I sense that any moment they will come for us, and that this time, there will be no Christian to protect us, and the true monsters will rip out our hearts and drink our blood, and there won't be a damn thing I can do about it.

~

Her entries read like a horror story, this macabre love affair between my mother and the two vampires in the photo—Christian Du Mauré and his best friend Michel Baptiste. Who has names like those? I glance again at the photo of the two of them. How could vampires be real?

Yet here they are.

I can only assume they posed in the photograph for my mother.

Reading about the death of her brother Ryan makes me cringe. No wonder she never spoke about him. He'd been giving his blood to vampires for money? I have to reread this entry twice to believe it. *But why?*

On the other hand … my mother, talking about vampires.

I all but run to the front door, make sure that it and all the windows are locked. Once satisfied, I return to my chair, and her journal.

I look again at the photograph.

Is it my imagination, or do the men pictured seem like grown, animated dolls, all porcelain skin and dark eyes?

I skip back several entries and read another, from earlier in time.

~

I held my son in my arms for the first time today. Julien Ryan Perretti was born at 12:14 a.m., here in this cottage, on December 31, 2010. He is healthy, with a head of dark hair and light eyes. All I remember is a flush of liquid running down my legs and Michel guiding me to bed. Perhaps it was my vampire blood, or perhaps knowing that I was bringing a life into this world, but I swear I felt no pain. When Michel handed my son to me, he and I cried. For me, it was bittersweet, and I wonder if Michel felt the same.

I put Julien to my breast and relaxed while Michel collected the bloody sheets. He swore he had never delivered a child before, but to have remained ignorant his entire long life? I had to wonder. As Julien nursed, a million disconnected thoughts ran through my mind, yet I felt at peace. I had a son, and no matter his true father, I was his mother. My life was no longer mine alone but would forever belong to him.

When I felt myself drifting off, I gave my son to Michel, who swaddled and held Julien as if he were his own son. I had thought of Michel as so ill-prepared to be a father, when in fact he was a natural, a being who I thought loved no one more than himself. But I saw the love he felt for Julien, and I knew we were safe. Only then was I able to drift off to sleep.

When I woke, Michel was sitting on the edge of my bed, again cradling Julien in his arms. I could feel the sun dancing on my skin. Without speaking, I offered Michel my wrist, for I needed him to stay awake. He took just enough to give himself the strength to resist the coming sun. I held Julien to my breast again, the movement both natural and comforting.

I would have killed anyone who tried to harm my son.

Michel wrapped his arms around me and held me close while I nursed Julien. Fear, happiness, and love raced through me like fire.

Neither of us spoke of Christian, though I felt him between with us.

~

I try to imagine my mother lying in bed with this beautiful dark-haired vampire, nursing me and loving Michel while missing Christian. They were quite the family, my mother and her two vampire lovers. It appears I owe Michel a debt I might never be able to repay. If only I could thank him for all he did for us.

Other entries enlighten me to her life. Occasionally, she wrote about missing New York and her job at the Metropolitan Museum of Art. She left everything behind and fled to California, where I truly think she believed they would be safe. That is, until she wrote, "The three of us literally packed up and boarded a plane one evening for Paris." They had been living "like fugitives," as she put it, hiding from another vampire named Josette Delacore, a woman who had been alive during the French Revolution.

I read farther.

~

I had a dream about Christian being held against his will, somewhere in France. We have narrowed the place down to the Château des Singes—the house of monkeys. It lies in ruins somewhere west of Paris. Michel won't speak of the debauchery he witnessed there in eighteenth-century France.

Was Christian there, too?

Whoever lured Christian back to Paris is now holding him hostage. I believe Josette Delacore has something to do with it. I know that she was made vampire and that she shadowed their lives for centuries. Perhaps she needed to get Christian away from us in the hopes that

Michel would follow, too, leaving Julien and me at her
mercy. She hates me and will kill us at the first opportunity.
> *But I'll kill her before I ever let her harm my son.*
> *Something has scared Michel. I can see it in his eyes,*
though he denies it.

~

I reread it all again, right to the page where my
mother recounts sitting on an airplane fleeing to Paris. Then I
turn to the last page. There, in her small, neat penmanship,
my mother left a note.

> *Julien—if you are reading this, I am dead.*
> *You must text this telephone number and leave only*
> *this message: "Amanda is dead. Please come." The*
> *vampire who receives this message has been to the*
> *manor many times, so he does not need to be invited*
> *inside, but you must make him identify himself. He is*
> *the dark-haired man in the photo. His name is Michel*
> *Baptiste, and only he is allowed entry into this house.*
> <u>*Do not let anyone else inside—only him.*</u>
> *Trust him and listen to him in all things.*
> *That's all you need to do. Text that message*
> *and wait for him. I love you—Mom.*

~

My hands shake as I type and send the message.
Millions of divergent thoughts run through my mind. Am I
really texting a vampire and waiting for him to show up at
my door? The very same vampire who held me in his arms
and watched my mother nurse me? I try to imagine their
lives in California, what it was like, and fall asleep doing so.

* * *

Bang!
Something startles me awake. My cell phone tells me
it's one in the morning.
Another *bang* echoes through the house. Perhaps my
text has been answered! I jump from the chair and run for the
front door. Who will be waiting?

Despite my best efforts, my hands shake as I turn the lock. With no way to prepare myself, my tension almost boils over. Still, my mother trusted this man. And he saved both our lives, not once but twice. I take a deep breath, swing open the massive front door, and come face to face with a presence standing on the gravel walkway, lit by the quarter moon.

Dressed entirely in black, he stands as if posing for a photo shoot. I do a double-take. He's wearing a short mink coat and knee-high boots, and his hair falls around his shoulders, just as in the photograph. In fact, nothing about him has changed at all. Perhaps he can't change, like a being frozen in time.

I open my mouth to speak, but before I can form the words to ask him who the hell he is, he pushes past me into the foyer.

Chapter 33
Julien

The figure is handsome—no, beyond handsome. Beautiful. Although attired in the eccentric outfit, he fits well in this house, but would fit better in the eighteenth century. He smiles, and his emerald eyes lighten. His skin is pale, textured like that of a sculpture, smooth and almost translucent.

He appears to float to the living room, where he begins to gracefully rekindle the embers in the fireplace.

I watch, open-mouthed and speechless.

Finally, he stands, apparently satisfied with the roaring blaze. Casually, he slips off his coat and drops it onto one of the sofas. Underneath, he wears a sort of sheer black T-shirt and lots of silver jewelry—necklaces, bracelets, and rings.

"Ah, it's been a long time …" He looks around. "Nothing much has changed, though. Still a museum."

I manage to find my voice. "May I ask your name?"

He takes a seat in my mother's favorite chair and studies me, his fingers playing through his hair.

My hands are sweaty again. I wipe them on my pants. "I'm sorry, I have to ask. It was in her …" I collapse on the couch myself, at a loss for words.

"I am Michel." He smiles. "Your mother and I had a pact. I promised I would not come until she was … until I received your text."

"You got here so quickly … how?"

Clearly ignoring me, he says, "Now, where to begin?" and rubs his hands together. "You might want to get comfortable. This is going to take some time."

I lift my glass from the side table. "Some Cognac, perhaps?"

He laughs, and I relax and lean back into the couch.

"Has anyone been by to see you?" Michel asks.

"You mean, like, our neighbors?"

"No, no. I mean, any strangers coming by asking about *her*. Anyone like *me*?"

I shake my head.

"Well, they will."

This does call for more to drink. I get up, pour a shot, knock it back, refill my tumbler, and return to the couch. "My mother said not to let anyone else in. I assumed she meant anyone not human."

"You always were a fast learner."

"Who are *they*, and how would they hear about her death? I haven't had time to put a legal notice in the papers."

He shrugs. "Believe me, *they* will find out. May I ask how she died?"

"She was found in the woods—"

"The clearing?"

I nod. "Apparently, she was lying there as if she had just fallen asleep. The neighbors said there were no marks or bruises on her. I assumed she had a heart attack. What else could kill such a young woman?"

"The question is not what but who would kill her, Julien?" He falls silent, still staring at me. "God, you look so much like your father."

Then it dawns on me. I shove the photograph at him. "You knew my father?"

"Oh, God, where did you find this?" He studies the photograph closely, shaking his head.

"In with my mother's journal. That's you and my father, isn't it?"

A smile slowly emerges. "Yes, that is me, on the right. The curmudgeon on the left is your father, my best friend, Christian Du Mauré."

Though he is eternally my age, I finally have proof that my father existed. "He's beautiful."

Michel nods. "Beautiful, agreed; impossible, very."
He hands me back the photograph.

"My mother never spoke of him," I say. "In fact, I
know about five things about him, and … Wait. He's *still*
your best friend, which means … he's alive? She never
spoke about either of you. Why?" My heart is pounding.
Finally, I've met someone who knew him—who *knows* him.
"We lived alone in this time capsule, but she never said … I
mean, I never brought him up, and from the little she said, I
sensed that she loved him, but there was such sadness in her
voice."

"Oh my, it's so complicated, Julien. How old are you
now?"

"I'll be twenty-one on—"

"New Year's Eve." He nods. "I remember."

"I read about you in my mother's journal. You and
my mother—"

"I know you have many questions, but there is much
I can tell you that will put many things into perspective. May
I begin now, and you save your questions until the end? That
would be the most logical way to reach our goal."

"Which is?"

"To keep you alive until morning."

"I definitely need another Cognac." But I find I'm
not afraid of the truth. I want to know it all, every sordid
detail. "Is my father really still alive?"

"Yes, he is very much alive, but your mother has
spent her life shielding you from all of us. She wanted never
to draw any attention to you."

I look at my watch. After one-thirty in the morning.
"How much time do we have?"

"About seven hours. Then you must come with me,
Julien. You will no longer be safe in this house."

"Not *safe?*" I shoot to my feet. The room sways
around me. The photo slips from my hand.

Michel grabs my elbow and steadies me.

I swallow hard. "I think I feel sick."

"This is no time to fall apart, Julien. I held you in my arms when you were an infant. I made sure you and your mother stayed safe. She gave up her life to make sure nothing would ever happen to you, so you must be strong. Do you understand me?"

I think I nod. "Why would anyone want to kill me?"

"Sit down and listen. What I tell you will seem unbelievable, but I swear, all of it is true." He crosses himself, and we both sit down. "Where to begin …?" He sighs, picking up the photo once more.

Chapter 34
Julien

After a long pause, Michel begins to speak. "Christian and I were both born in the year 1737 and made vampire twenty years later, in the year of our Lord 1757. We grew up not far from here in what then was the village of Meudon, near the palace of Versailles. Your father and I were best friends from the time we could walk and talk, and we never wavered in our loyalty to one another.

"Change came in the form of a beautiful mortal girl. Her name was Josette Delacore. She was married to a minor aristocrat and had become the mistress of a vampire who hated both Christian and me with a passion.

"To ... simplify things ... we three became lovers and, within three years, Josette had a child—Solange, a beautiful little girl with dark wavy hair and green eyes. As all this was happening, what you call the French Revolution was brewing as aristocrats fled Paris for London and other European cities. I cannot describe the fear, chaos and panic as society broke down, families turned against one another, paranoia reigned. Fearing their arrest, Josette asked Christian to take the child and give her to a family that could provide for her. Reluctantly, he did, for many French families were fleeing to England. He had no difficulty finding one to take the child."

He pauses again. I sip my Cognac, almost afraid to speak in case I should ruin his train of thought.

Michel continues. "We debated whether or not to turn Josette into one of us, to give her the gift of eternal life and have her with us forever, but your father felt that it was not his gift to give. He would not interfere in the world of mortals.

"The last time we saw Josette, she had given Christian all her jewels, which we needed to survive. We boarded a ship—*Le Cométe*, I believe it was called—and headed to London without looking back. God, what a shit hole that ship was. I'm surprised we survived the journey.

"Before we bedded down that first night on board, Christian opened the jewelry box and found, embedded among all her jewels, a note. In it, Josette explained that Solange was his daughter, not her mortal husband's child, as we had been led to believe. At that moment, your father vowed to watch over her while she remained alive, yet also to keep his distance. He wanted her to have a normal life.

"I remember laughing when he told me, at the irony of it all, for you see, Christian only ever wanted to be a husband and a father. He had been in love with my sister Leila and had sworn he would marry her, until she was married off to another. He had wanted to stay in Meudon and raise a family. That was all he had ever asked for, and now he had a child whom he would never know, who was mortal, and who would grow old and die while he—Christian— remained imprisoned in the body of a twenty-year-old boy.

"But Christian vowed to keep her safe, for though he had given Solange a new home with a mortal family, he thought of her forever afterward as his child. I was the only one who knew her true parentage. We were young, yes, but we knew that the child of a mortal and a vampire was a rare thing, so we told no one, for fear she would be killed." Michel sighs. "Sometimes I wish she had been killed, for although she grew up a privileged woman in London, she was so full of hatred that she could not be stopped."

"What became of her?" Trembling, I asked, "Did she die?"

He rises and walks over to the fireplace. "No. She was made a vampire by Gaétan—"

"The vampire who was Josette's lover?"

"Yes, she became his lover." Michel's lips twist. "You see, Gaétan hated us, and his revenge was to turn Solange into a vampire as she lay dying of yellow fever in

London in 1814. He then took her back to Paris, and they became rulers of the vampire world. He poisoned her mind with talk of how Christian was her father yet had abandoned her. She believed it, and her hatred of Christian grew and grew."

I clear my throat. "Are you all so … mean-spirited?"

Michel sits back down on the couch and laughs. "No, Julien. Vampires don't change very much. Yes, we can read minds or become extremely strong, and some can fly, I imagine, but you never lose your basic personality." He pauses. "Christian and I had a bond that could never have been broken, an unspoken agreement that we would never turn a mortal into one of us. Instead, we chose to escape the mores and customs of a time or place and move on so we could hide in plain sight. That's why New York was so appealing. We lived there successfully for the longest time."

"If you liked New York so much, why did you leave?"

"You're getting ahead of yourself, but if you must know the truth, three things happened to set in motion the wheels that bring us to tonight."

I find I have to move. In spite of the sweat running down my neck, I get up to toss more logs on the fire, though the blaze we have is large enough to last for hours. I'm torn between trying to digest the story, and a certain twisted relief. My mother's behavior finally begins to make sense to me.

Michel gives me a nod as I retake my seat. "The vampire Gaétan came to New York to find your mother, who was working at the Metropolitan Museum of Art at the time. She had a wonderful career, and next to you, I would guess she loved her work the most.

"Gaétan fell in love with her. Instead of following through with his plan to slaughter her, he wanted her for himself. You see, your mother was very special. It was her blood."

Her blood? I stare at him. "She was very private," I say slowly, "but I always knew what she was thinking. … Well, at least, I thought I did, but sometimes she had a strange look in her eyes, and she never seemed to age. She ate very little—"

"Stop, Julien. Your mother was not a vampire, although she was possessed of vampire blood, and she is a descendant of *the* Josette Delacore, who was a powerful psychic and witch in her day. Like Josette's blood did, your mother's blood calls out to vampires with a scent and a song that is seductive. Haunting." Michel shakes his head. "I know of no vampire who could refuse Josette anything. Your mother, on the other hand, chose not to use her gifts. She wanted to live a normal life. That is why she ended up here. She loved Christian dearly, even when he abandoned her … but I get ahead of myself."

The confirmation—that my father did abandon my mother—simmers inside me, but I've latched onto something else Michel said earlier. "What was the plan Gaétan and Solange had for my mother?"

He slaps both hands on his knees. "Picture a group of vampires living in Paris for hundreds of years. They are beautiful and wealthy yet almost medieval in their thinking. They still believe in kings and queens, subjects and slavery of sorts. Our maker Gabrielle, and Gaétan, were this kind of vampire. Word made its way back to them about your mother and her powerful blood. She was deemed a threat to our kind, so several vampires came to New York to destroy her.

"Your father, who had watched over Solange and all her offspring through the centuries, was watching over your mother. He saved her life and brought the wrath of Solange upon her, for Solange had lost Gaétan to your mother. Solange was jealous, especially with Amanda pregnant and the child's paternity in question."

"But you told me Christian was my father."

"That is true, but at the time, it was not known whether Christian had fathered you or if Gaétan—"

"My mother had an affair with him, too?"

"Ah, yes. She did, but when Gaétan came for her, Christian killed him in Central Park."

"How does one kill a vampire?" I read some of my mother's books about vampires, but I never believed any of it.

Then again, I never had occasion to believe it before.

Michel sits back on the couch. "He beheaded him."

That explains my mother's journal entry about the vampire in Central Park who killed her brother. Then Christian, my father, had killed the vampire—Gaétan.

"Holy shit."

"Yes, it was quite a sight to witness your father wield a machete." Michel smiles. "It was rare, but when he did …" He shakes his head. "After Gaétan died, Solange came to New York, hunting for your mother. Obviously, she did not succeed in killing her. I assume Solange returned to Paris, but I have not heard a word about her in decades. She could be dead, for all I know."

"Why did my father abandon my mother? Did he not love her?" For heaven's sake, I sound like a pathetic child. I wish I could retract my words. Sure, a life with a father—okay, a vampire father—would have been a bit strange, but in many ways, his absence filled our house and controlled our lives.

Michel nods. "Your mother was a wise woman. She knew that Christian loved her, but she also knew that he had never lost hope that Josette had survived prison and the guillotine. Even when I produced a death certificate—"

"You got a death certificate?"

"No … in truth, it was faked, to placate him." Michel sighs. "Still, he wondered about her. Your mother never believed that Josette had died, and they were connected by blood, along with many gifts that they shared by the very nature of that blood. When Christian got it in his head that Josette was alive and living in Paris, he left your mother and me to find out."

"Was my mother right?"

"Unfortunately, she was, Julien." He stares into the fire, and at the look on his face, I dare not bring myself to interrupt him with another question.

After a long moment, Michel continues. "One night, our town house in New York burned to the ground. We were not home, but we lost literally everything, so we fled to California. We found a small cottage in Venice Beach, near the ocean, and I opened a club there, which I called Michel's. Sometimes your mother came to visit me there, while I was working. She was pregnant, and very lonely. We were both in shock over losing Christian. She used to wait while I tended bar.

"You see, I never lost my need to be amongst mortals. Your father had hated humanity and really wished to be left alone, but I needed to mingle among mortals yet keep you both safe. Opening a club was the perfect intersection of those two worlds for me.

"Your mother kept dreaming about Christian, and insisting she'd seen him in the club. I dismissed it as her loneliness. Don't misunderstand me—I missed him, as well, but I never saw him, not once. It was such a confusing, lonely time for the two of us. We were adrift, trying to piece together some semblance of a life, to make order from the chaos of having lost Christian, our home, and our sense of purpose.

"Slowly, our lives became more routine, and we had adjusted to living in California until one night at the club, when everything changed forever."

Chapter 35
Julien

As I listen to Michel, his rich accent and softly turned phrases, I try to imagine it all: ancient beings, vampires, witches. Words and phrases like "New World," chatelaines, and my father "assuming the throne."

I'm finding it too much to absorb, and I guess Michel notices, for he started speaking louder. "Julien. Stay with me."

Before I can respond, he slits his palm with a silver dagger and pushes it against my face. "Drink, and you'll be fine."

His blood smears my skin, but I try to move my head. He's stronger and keeps his hand against me. "Just a taste," he says. "I promise you will not get sick."

I keep trying to pull away, but suddenly, something tastes sweet, and I realize I am tasting his blood. It's not so bad. I close my eyes and lick again.

As his blood coats my throat, I find myself becoming aroused, and then unable to pull away. Heat fills my face in shame. I've been with girls before, but this is such a bizarre experience. As I latch onto his hand, something clicks inside me.

He caresses my hair, whispering, "That's it. Easy does it."

Even so, my mind is working. I am the son of a vampire and a woman who had magical blood. That's how I knew things about my mother without being told. Why school was embarrassingly easy for me, why my mother did not need to tell me things because I knew her thoughts.

Why, the night she was in the clearing with Michel, I was not fazed by it—why I watched in awe, not horror.

Why so many of her books were about subjects like the French Revolution, vampires, witchcraft and time travel, the ancient history of Paris and the French monarchy. She had books on tarot cards, psychometry, palm reading, crystals, and numerology. She stashed issues of *National Geographic*, and history books on the Picts and ancient Romans. She devoured everything on the subjects of eighteenth-century France, the catacombs, London, and the American West. I never understood why.

But these subjects were not merely her interests. They comprised her entire life and were her way of understanding the world into which she had been thrust.

Just as Michel pulls his hand away, I see my mother's face in my mind's eye.

He wipes my mouth with his sleeve. "There, you look better now. You had that chalky vampire pallor."

I'm not really listening. "I saw her, my mother … I saw her in your blood."

He nods. "Your mother had very powerful blood. When I needed to walk in the daylight, she would sometimes give me a taste. Are you all right?"

I draw a deep breath and try to calm myself. "I think so. I don't know what happened to me. It was like I was losing my sense of reality."

"It's called shock, Julien." Michel kisses me gently on the cheek like a parent rewards a child. "We still have much to talk about tonight."

I lick my lips. "I saw you both in the clearing one night, when I was just a boy."

He sits back down in my mother's chair but says nothing.

I continue, sweat gathering on my palms. "My mother sometimes went out for walks in the woods. I always worried about her, but she never seemed afraid. She told me that walking cleared her head. One spring night, I must have had a bad dream, which I sometimes did, but I went to her room, and her bed was empty. I knew she had to be out in the woods, so I took a risk and followed her.

"I remember the quarter moon shedding just enough light for me to see. I was forbidden to ever go into the woods after sunset. I never knew why, but I never broke her rule until that night.

"The sky was clear, and I smelled spring—you know, earth and growth and life. Well, as I parted the trees for the clearing, I saw her with what I thought was another woman. They were lying naked together in the grass, kissing one another. Just when I thought I had seen enough, the woman pulled away from my mother, and I realized it wasn't a woman at all, but a man—my mother's lover. He bent his head and latched onto her neck.

"When he let go, blood ran down her neck, but they stayed entwined. It was at that moment that I knew my mother was not of this world, that she was something *other*, though I had no idea what she could be. Vampires, to me, were creatures of the night that slept in coffins. My mother was always home during the day; she ate food and drank wine, slept in a regular bed. I wondered if the creature could be my father, but as I watched them tangled together, I knew I could never speak of it to her."

I stop, but Michel doesn't move. I can still taste his blood on my lips. "That was you with my mother that night, wasn't it?"

He nods but says nothing.

"So you two were lovers, despite your best friend being my father?"

"Julien, your mother and I had a complicated relationship. Christian had demanded that I stay in New York with her to protect her from harm, which I did willingly. The night our town
house burned, everything changed for us. We were running for our lives, Christian was gone, and I suppose our love for Christian drove us into one another's arms. It sounds like a

cliché, I know, but by then she was pregnant, and I could not abandon her. So we literally fled wearing only our clothes and settled in Venice Beach."

I hesitate to ask— *Do I really want to know his answer?*—but … "Did you love my mother?"

He pauses and stares so long into the fire that I'm not sure he heard me.

Then he turns, his eyes a lighter green. He appears more human, warmer, as if filled with sunshine. "Your mother was smart, loyal, and extremely brave. She had not asked for any of what happened, yet she faced all of it with courage. Did I love her? Yes, very much, but was I *in love* with her? No. Do you understand the difference?"

"Then why were you fucking her?" I'm on my feet again, pacing and trying to unclench my fists, to decide why I'm angry. They were bonded by history—isn't that what holds most couples together? I take a breath. "I'm sorry, Michel. That was rude of me."

"No apologies necessary. You see, circumstances did not allow us to walk away from one other. We both felt abandoned by Christian, don't forget. We were wounded and lost without him, and so we turned to one another. We were islands for one another in a sea of grief, bound together by our love for your father and by the hope that he would return to us so that we three could carry on together again.

"When you both moved into this house, Victor made me swear to stay away, and for five years, I avoided both you and your mother. It was enough time for Victor to lose interest in you, and life, as they say, goes on, and so I returned to you.

"I am almost three hundred years old, Julien. I have seen much that makes me weep, but the fact that your mother and I could keep you alive this long is a testament to us both. A miracle, really, considering that Victor could have destroyed us all as easily as swat flies. Why he left your mother, and then all of us, alone is beyond me."

"So who was Victor?" Another question I am afraid to ask yet to which I must know the answer.

"You are a glutton for punishment." He smiles weakly.

Chapter 36
Julien

"As it turns out," Michel says, "Victor proved a double-edged sword. I can only assume he pursued me, for one night months later, your mother and I were walking home—you were with us—and he came out of nowhere. It was awkward, to say the least, and though Victor had eyes only for your mother, he watched you carefully, as well … and for lack of a better way to say it, they fell in love. No, don't look at me that way. I'm just telling you the truth. He saw her and was smitten. It was obvious that she was intrigued by him, too. Julien, you must understand, in him she found the ultimate protector, for you see, Victor was not like Christian or myself.

"I learned much about Victor over the years, and one of the things he spoke to me about was his heritage. He had been made vampire centuries ago, at a time when Europe was struggling to rebuild after the Romans were defeated and went home with their spears between their legs."

"What happened to him?" I glance at my watch. It's half past three in the morning.

Michel shakes his head. "I'm really not sure. He had power, true power, and he loved your mother for a time. He gave her this house for the two of you, stayed around for perhaps five years, and then vanished. I have no idea where he is. Maybe he went back to the catacombs. He was a member of a group of vampires known as the Ancient Ones, for in their world, Victor was but a child, though, like me, he loved mortal women, and he seemed to like me. I mean, he left me alive when he could have slaughtered me and done God knew what to you and your mother.

"I had to leave you both—that was the deal he struck with your mother. Once you both were gone, I was … free. I don't mean that you and your mother were a burden, but

Victor had taken control of her life, and I was left to roam
Paris and renew my love for the weaker sex."

"Didn't you miss us?"

He smiles and brushes my cheek with a cold hand. "I
did, I truly did, but I had promised Victor I would stay away.
At the time, I could not understand why, but later I realized
that he was protecting all of us."

"From whom? I don't understand. You're a vampire.
Aren't you omnipotent?"

Michel laughs, and sobers. "Victor had sometimes
spoken of a being far older and wiser than himself, one who
had no use for vampires. Someone not too integrated into the
modern world. He was known to me as Captain Andreas.
He's no one with whom to interfere, but technically he is
your grandfather—"

"My grandfather?"

"Yes, he was Christian's true father—not that bastard
who raised him. A true asshole if there ever was one."

I must look confused, because Michel says, "Let me
explain. Captain Andreas lay with a mortal woman and begot
your father. Christian's mother, your grandmother, died at a
very young age of the pox and is buried on the grounds of
their home in Meudon. Captain Andreas has spent the last
several hundred years watching over Christian and protecting
him from all sorts of ugliness."

"Can't we turn to him for protection?"

"He's not convinced you are Christian's son, Julien."

"How do you know that? Have you spoken to him?"

"When Christian's mother died—we were only eight
years old, but we discovered him in her bedroom rummaging
through her meager personal belongings. He loved her so
much. Only later would we learn how he protected the two
of us from God knew what. I am convinced we made it
through the French Revolution and out of Paris thanks only
to his intervention. We were young and arrogant, and by

rights, we should have been slaughtered by our own kind, but he protected us and kept us safe."

"So, maybe he will help us now?"

"No, no, Julien." Michel shakes his head. "He sees you as nothing but a problem to be eradicated in his scheme of ruling the world. Yes, nothing more than a bug to stamp out."

Chapter 37
Michel

2030—La Maison des Rêves

Julien looked so tired and fragile, but I knew he was
strong. One day, he would know the total truth about his
father. Perhaps it would take him experiencing love for
himself to truly understand what two people would do in the
name of love and responsibility.

It was growing late. Although sunrise was a few
hours away, I could feel warmth in the air. The fire had
burned down to embers, and it was no use stoking it up
again, for we would not remain here much longer.

Nothing had changed in this so-called house of
dreams, for it had been the perfect home for Amanda, even
better suited to her personality than the Upper East Side
town house Christian and I had shared with her in
Manhattan, or our house in Le Marais. This place was a
comfortable museum, and that was always the place where
Amanda had belonged. She'd loved working in the Met, and
here, she'd been surrounded by priceless antiques and books,
her two favorite pleasures in life.

"So this Victor fellow," Julien said. "He was working
to save my mother and me, yet he was friends with this
Captain Andreas?"

I nodded. "Yes, he kept his relationship with your
mother a secret."

"Did you ever go to the Château des Singes,
Michel?" Julien was suddenly alert, as if he knew it was
almost time to leave this place yet still wanted to hear more.

I had hoped to avoid this part of the story, and I
would have never brought it up, but he had, and so I had to
finish the tale, leaving nothing out.

Well, sort of …

"Well." I paused, running a hand through my hair. I stared past him. How to best tell him? "I was there, Julien, only once."

"So you saw my father?" He leaned towards me.

"After your mother left ... I remained in our house in the Marais. For a time, I was lost without her, for my days and nights had revolved around protecting you both, making sure you were never alone. ... You know, I've told all this to you.

"Anyway, it was clear that your mother loved Victor, and he clearly wanted her, but I guess I held out hope that they would fall apart, or that something someday would drive her back to me."

"It sounds awful." Julien frowned as he leaned back on the sofa.

"It was very sad for a very long time. I wandered the streets of Paris, looking for ... I don't know, another vampire to bond with, comfort, debauchery. It was all there, though I guess I wasn't as keen on it as I had thought, for going to clubs no longer held much allure for me, and as for women, I was back to my old—or should I say, *younger* ways, when women were something to use, to occupy my nights. It was not even about the blood anymore, for I was closing in on three hundred years old. I needed little blood.

"I was lonely, and it was only with the absence of you both that I realized how much I needed and loved you. Amanda and I had been through so much together. She was strong, responsible, intact, and she had grounded me, as had you, for I felt such a sense of duty to you two.

"These were foreign feelings for me. They were adult, moral feelings, the likes of which I had never experienced in my life. Your father had always been the responsible one, which had enabled me to run wild with no thought except for my own needs. He was light-years ahead of me, for he was the ultimate in responsibility and duty.

"But ironically, he'd been the one who had left Amanda and me in New York and come here. He was the one who had thrown away all that he'd had for a memory, a lost love. How responsible was that? … Yet he was also my history. More than my best friend, he was the reminder, the validation of all I once was as a mortal man, living in another time and place."

I continued. "You see, Julien, time passes. Our loved ones die, and all that was familiar, that made us who we are, is gone. Your history lives and dies with you, but we never die … yet the world changes, and we either adapt or go mad. There is no middle ground."

It was with that realization that I finally understood Christian, for his actions had forced me to assume his role and be the rock, the rational, loyal one. I had always wondered what it felt like to be there for another person. I supposed his leaving had set me on a course that, as corny as it sounded, made me grow up. I'd thought that I was the only vampire who could protect Amanda and Julien, and though I had saved them from Josette Delacore, I felt as though I had driven Amanda right into the arms of someone so powerful that she could not deny him anything.

"What happened to you?" Julien brought me back to the present. "Where did you go?"

"Probably ten years had passed when I noticed an envelope on the front porch when I came home one fall morning." I flashed back to when Christian and I were living in London and I discovered the note left by Josette Delacore.

I panicked and almost burned it, but my curiosity had overridden my better judgement. How had she found me again? God, it was déjà vu all over again.

"It was actually an invitation," I said slowly. "An eighteenth-century masquerade ball was being held at the Château des Singes on Halloween night, and I was invited."

I thought Julien would jump off the couch. His face became more animated. "Who sent it? Christian?"

"Here's the kicker." I laughed, remembering clearly. "Who knows who really wrote it, but the invitation was signed *Christian and His Court*."

"His court? Like court of law?" Julien scratched his head.

"No, like a royal court … kings and queens." I made the motion of a crown on my head.

"Kings and queens … how strange."

"Julien, it was beyond strange, but of course, I had to go. It was being held on Halloween night, which was only a week away, and I needed a costume, so I rented one of those eighteenth-century get-ups, which were much like the clothing we'd actually worn. I purchased a powered wig and a black mask, and I was—"

"How did you know it was safe? I mean, they knew where you lived. What if it hadn't been a party but was a trap, instead?"

"I didn't know either way, but someone had taken the time to seek me out and invite me, and in my world, one did not turn down an invitation from royalty."

Chapter 38
Michel

Julien was glowing with anticipation. But how could I tell him the truth of what I had witnessed that Halloween night in 2020, as my carriage had approached the Château des Singes?

In that instant, I made a choice. I could not tell him what had really happened, and so I made up a happier tale.

"Well," I began, "I actually donned clothing I had owned in the eighteenth century, adding a black mask and a powdered white wig. I was quite the picture of eighteenth-century glamour. I could not believe I was there again, in the foyer of the Château des Singes, hobnobbing with vampires dressed in silk gowns and white wigs. Beautiful music echoed off the marble walls of the ballroom, which held two hundred people, easily. It was a sea of vampires, none of whom I knew, so I found a place to stand, hoping to see either Christian or Josette.

"I was so excited that if I had had a beating heart, it would have been racing. Still, I could not focus. Mortal women tried to engage me in conversation, and I found myself being led to the ballroom by a zaftig woman in a deep red gown. I even tried to focus on her huge bosom, but it was no use. I could think only of Christian and Josette.

"As I turned the corner to enter the ballroom, another hand took mine and led me into the mélange of silk and sweat and blood. We turned to face one another, but I already knew that it could only have been one person—my former lover and recent nemesis, Josette Delacore.

"She curtsied, and I bowed, and we danced an eighteenth-century court dance. Funny how some things never leave us. She smiled as we moved as one around the vast room, surrounded by satin and power, and my God, I was transported back in time. The steps of the gavotte came back to me effortlessly.

"I thought back to our last meeting in California. It was such a stark contrast. I kept looking around for Christian, for my guess was that he was watching us from the shadows.

"As she turned into my arms, Josette slipped an envelope into my trouser pocket. 'Where is he?' I whispered, but she ignored me. When the dance ended, she slipped into the crowds.

"Did I dare to open the note there? I thought better of it, and so I made my way out of the ballroom and dashed down a hallway, where I found myself in the library. It truly was Christian's dream come true. The room was massive, and I could easily imagine him sitting there for hours on end, reading his books alone, lost in thought.

"I opened the envelope, keeping my eyes on the doorway. The note said only, *Turn around.* It was signed with the letter C.

"Christian himself moved from the shadows, passing the ornate furniture and mirrors, still the most beautiful thing in the room—in fact, in *this* room." I gestured around us, drawing Julien's attention back to our surroundings, and continued. "The fire from each massive fireplace cast a bronze glow across him, as though he were in full sunlight. His blond hair was shoulder-length, tied back with a ribbon that matched his gold trousers, shoes, and frock coat. He wore no mask. He was alone, as far as I could tell, and I—"

"How did he look?" Julien interrupted me. "How did my father appear to you?"

"Well, though it had only been twenty years since I had last seen him, at that moment it felt like a lifetime. I choked on my words. Then he smiled, and though they were rare, when your father smiled, it was genuine.

"'Christian,' I said, 'or should I call you Your Majesty?'"

"He grasped both my hands. 'You look well, my friend.'

"'You mean, despite the wig.' I pulled at a strand of it. 'God, how did they wear these things?'

"His laughter echoed through the room, God, how I'd missed him. Then he turned serious again. "Oh Michel, how I regret coming back here.'"

"His confession almost bowled me over, but he held onto me.

"'I miss you so much. I am so sorry Michel.'

"It felt, Julien, as though no time had passed between us. It was like that with us." I paused, remembering. Twenty years had seemed like nothing at all. Christ, I had locked him up in a coffin for a longer period of time than that.

"'How is Amanda?' Christian finally asked me.

"'She is well, Christian. Her son ... your son, Julien, is twenty now and is in college.'

"He pulled me closer. 'Where can I find her?'

"'She lives in Villepreux, in a place called La Maison des Rêves.'

"'House of dreams,' he mused. 'Hmm. How did she end up ... there?'

"'A vampire named Victor,' I told him. "'He and she became ... He set her up there many years ago.'

"His eyes darkened at the mention of Victor, but I'd had to tell him the truth. 'And you?'

"'I live in the Marais, alone. ... And you are the king.' As I spoke, I felt something pressed into my right hand.

"'Yes,' Christian said, 'I am king, and I command that you leave here, never to return. Do you understand me?'

"His face was serious, but I could not take him seriously. Something was up, yet I had to play my part.

"'Of course, Your Majesty.' I knelt, feeling like a total dork.

"'On pain of death,' he said, 'you must never return here again.'

"I then rose, nodded, and turned away, fighting so many feelings, the least of them fear, for I guessed that Josette had been hiding in the shadows, listening to us. As I turned, I slipped the object he'd given me into my coat pocket.

"How is it," I mused aloud, almost forgetting Julien's presence, "that the past never truly leaves us, but linger in our hearts and minds forever? Seeing him was both so familiar and so foreign, as if a gulf had split open between us, a chasm that could never again be mended, and yet he had been my best friend since we were mortal children. I quickly took my leave, not wanting him to see my tears.

"I felt for the small box in my coat pocket as I crossed the lawn outside, just to make sure I still had it. Impulsively, I pulled it out while I waited for a carriage to take me back to Paris. It was a matchbook.

"There in the moonlight, it all came rushing back: fighting with Christian over the design on the matchbook. We had debated putting the club name or even the address on it. He'd wanted less, of course, and I had always wanted more, so we'd settled on a black box with the grey outline of a wolf's face and, in red, the words *Bleeker Street*."

It had been our refuge, the intersection where mortals and vampires could meet and I could feel human again. Our club in the village.

The Grey Wolf.

Chapter 39
Michel

I paused in my tale and glanced at my watch: 4:30 a.m.

"Michel, when was the last time you actually saw my mother?" Julien asked, from the sofa.

I had moved closer to the fireplace. There were only embers now, reminding me that we'd all but run out of time. I picked up a Limoges figurine off a nearby shelf, as if the answer could be found somewhere on it. "About a week ago, actually, but she was not herself. In fact, she expressed her desire to return to New York."

"And leave me here alone?"

I shrugged. "You're in college now, Julien. I guess she felt that you were safe enough."

"Yeah, and now she's dead. Bad judgment." But he sounded truly remorseful for the first time tonight.

"Julien, listen to me. Don't ever doubt for a moment that we loved you and did everything in our power to protect you."

"But you couldn't protect her. Why not, Michel?"

I crossed the room and sat down beside him. "I know how bizarre this tale must seem to you," I said, "but I was forbidden to ever set foot here. It was only after your mother was sure Victor was out of the picture that I returned. My hands were tied, and besides, I'm sure Victor and Ghislain kept a watchful eye on you both."

"So she was planning to move all of this to New York?"

"No, Julien, Victor owns everything you see here. Your mother knew that, and probably would have taken only her clothing and journals, but now that she's … gone, be sure that Victor will be back to claim his bounty once again."

"Until the next mortal woman comes along for him to seduce and manipulate."

I nodded. "Could be. Still, Julien, we must leave soon. Do you understand?"

"Where to? My life is here and in Paris."

"You cannot return to Paris. It is a nest of vipers there. You must leave the country."

"I'm not going to California—no offense."

"None taken. I was thinking New York. I know some vampires there who may help us get settled."

"No kidding? New York. I always wanted to go there, but my mother refused to take me. Hey, I have my cell phone and my laptop. My passport is here. I don't have much money, though."

"Get yourself packed up. We head to Charles de Gaulle as soon as you are ready. The sooner we get out of France, the better I'll feel."

"Don't take this the wrong way, but why are you coming with me?"

"All I had here is gone. It's time for a change, and it's never too late to make a new go of things." I winked to reassure him and glanced at my Tag Hauer watch. "Please hurry now."

He left the room, and my smile faded from my face.

How could I have told him what had really happened when I'd gone to the masked ball ten years ago? That as I had approached in my carriage, I'd seen flames jutting through the night sky?

The smell of burning flesh, both mortal and vampire, had filled my senses that night. Screams had filled the darkness. There'd been vampires fleeing, carriages whirling past us, trying to get away from both burning buildings, engulfed in flames. I had jumped out the door of the carriage and run past the throngs of partygoers running for their lives.

I didn't remember even thinking that my best friend might not have survived. It was not an option.

Windows blew out all around me. Glass flew everywhere, slicing mortals in two. Their remains lay strewn on the lawn. It was a horror, an absolute horror.

I dodged chunks of brick from the chimneys, until I realized there was no house to run into—

"What happened?" I grabbed a man who was trying to pass me, shock on his face.

He said nothing and just kept moving.

I ran around the entire château, stopping at a smaller marble structure, which was thick with smoke. I had called out Christian's name until I'd had no voice left. Tears clouded my vision from the smoke, compounded by my own grief. Just as I made one more circle around the massive inferno, I had noticed Victor and Captain Andreas, hovering over something on the front lawn.

They had to have sensed me, for Victor ran towards me. "You must go, Michel," he had shouted. "He will slaughter you as well!"

"What happened here?" I shouted back over the roaring flames.

"Gabrielle, Josette … the boy … he burned them all and then set the house on fire. He has Christian, but he wants me to slaughter Amanda and her son," Victor gasped.

The look on my face must have scared him. "Who? Who burned them?"

"Don't worry, Michel." He touched my arm instead of answering me, apparently distracted from the mayhem around us. "I would never let anything happen to her. Go back to Paris and let me go to her."

"Let me go with—"

"No, please, I promise you. No harm will come to her. Just keep an eye out for the boy. Now go."

"Where is Christian? Just tell me, did he survive?"

"Barely," he whispered, and ran past me into the darkness, leaving me alone amidst rubble, bodies, and flames.

There was nothing more for me to do there. I'd had to trust that he would go back to La Maison des Rêves and find Amanda, and that he was telling me the truth about Christian. What other choice had I had?

Meanwhile, Julien just buried his mother. Did his father really survive the fire?

There was no way I could tell him about it.

I turned toward the stairs. "Julien, what are you doing up there? We have to go."

"Okay," he yelled from somewhere overhead.

Absentmindedly, I took up Amanda's journal from the coffee table, intending to make sure that Julien packed it, when a small envelope slipped out of the back sleeve and fell to the floor. I picked it up, shivering when I recognized my name on the back in her tiny handwriting.

A million thoughts ran through my head. Read it now? Pack it away until we were safely out of France?

I fondled the envelope and, being the impulsive soul that I am, tore it open while Julien scurried around upstairs. I sat back down on the couch to read it.

~

December 2010

Dear Michel,

I'll never forget the night Christian left us with only a note explaining why he had to return to Paris. It was the same night you told me that I was pregnant with the child of either Christian or Gaétan. Do you remember that night? It is one I will never forget, for Christian did not even have the decency to tell me himself, and I hated him for leaving us behind.

Now I am doing the same to you—only leaving behind a note to explain so much.

Later that same night I lost my baby. I will never know if it was the shock of learning that Christian had left me, or of learning that I was pregnant, or both. Anyway, I remember running upstairs with terrible cramps. I bled a bit. Then it was over. Shortly afterwards, I went to my doctor to make sure all was well, and although I was okay physically, I felt everything imaginable emotion: hate, fear, sadness, relief ... so many mixed emotions over being pregnant, losing my baby, losing Christian.

So, you see, Julien was never Christian's son.

Julien was conceived the night you and I fell into one another's arms, as if passion could have abated such agony and pain. He is your son, Michel.

When you helped deliver him and held his tiny, helpless body against your chest, how we both cried. I knew then that we both loved this child, no matter his true parentage, and that was when I fell in love with you. For the first time in a very long time, I felt safe, protected and valued. I was not sure up until the moment my water broke how I would get through his birth.

You kept me sane and grounded, and I love you for it, Michel. I know how much you hate sentiment—at least that's what you say—but you saved our lives so many times.

Withholding this truth from you kept our relationship ... uncomplicated, I guess would be the right word, and although we became lovers, I could never imagine being a parent alone. The thought was terrifying, Michel. Perpetuating this ruse was my ace in the hole, the only way to keep you by my side, for if I had told you the truth about Julien, you would have run like a frightened deer, and so playing this game was the only way it was possible to stay together and be a family.

Forgive me.
Love forever—Amanda.

She knew me better than I thought.

Chapter 40
Amanda

2030—La Maison des Rêves
Halloween

I stare out the kitchen window into the darkness, remembering how often I would walk out my back door here at La Maison des Rêves and into the woods to the clearing. In the beginning, Michel left a note in the planter just outside the door so I knew to wait until my son Julien was asleep. Then I would rush to meet him. My anticipation would build as I moved through the trees like some primal animal, my vampiric vision allowing me to glide easily in the utter darkness.

Tonight is Halloween, and the air sparks with magic and memories long passed. Julien is away at college in Paris, but when he was a child, I always feared getting caught.

As far as I know, though, my secret is still safe.

I have not seen Victor in five years, and I stopped expecting Michel. He comes as he needs to, and I'm fine with that.

I spent my life trying to keep Julien away from the ethereal world full of vampires, intrigue, and murder. It's a world I was thrust into with no understanding of the consequences. That happened twenty years ago, and though I could not have imagined the outcome, I have ended up here, in my eighteenth-century manor house, aptly called La Maison des Rêves—the house of dreams—hidden in the outskirts of Paris, left alone to raise my son.

Not a day passes that I do not think about Christian. I know he is somewhere in France, but I've long since given up the illusion that he'll come back to me, to us. Our love was short-lived yet intense, the most powerful experience of my life. Like Victor, all the vampires in my life left me, save one.

The mercurial, elusive Michel Baptiste remained my protector, friend, and lover. He kept his promise to Christian to watch over Julien and me and to keep us both safe. By the grace of God, he kept his word, and to this day I don't know how he managed it, but here we stayed out of the fray of the vampire wars that loomed all around us as they jockeyed for power and control.

Victor gave me the house, and still my blood boils when I relived the nights that he visited me here, enthralled with me, though I still don't know why. Ironically, my life was saved by one vampire, my son sired by another, and my life at the manor, a gift from a third. Perhaps I can say that I have been very fortunate, for though vampires are attracted to my blood, I try to live as normal a life as possible …

…until a note from Michel arrives, and then I can't get to the clearing soon enough to meet him. This routine started when Julien was just five years old and Victor was no longer in the picture, and Michel knew he would no longer incur Victor's wrath. We have played this game together for almost fifteen years now, which is nothing to Michel, who is almost three hundred years old.

Now, something makes me step outside into the fall air, which carries the scent of dying leaves and a hint of snow. It feels invigorating. I fantasize about Michel coming to me, but again, I can never predict it.

Still, I need to walk, and so I take the familiar path through the wood to the clearing.

Just as I arrive, moonlight breaks through the clouds and casts a bright light on the dying grass, surrounded by large boulders. I stop at the edge of the darkness, remembering all my trysts with Michel.

I'm scanning the trees when I see him coming towards me. I freeze. What could bring Victor to me after all these years?

He smells of smoke and burnt flesh. I search his face. Something is terribly wrong. "Victor, what is it?"

"There's been a fire at the Château des Singes—"

"Oh my God—Christian!"

His quick silence tells me everything. "He's alive, barely," he says quietly, "but Ghislain has gone mad, burning Josette, Gabrielle, and Mathieu, the boy, to death."

"Oh my God." I begin to tremble. "Was Christian burned?"

Victor shakes his head. "He tried to save them. … He's … I don't know … but you are no longer safe here. Ghislain demanded that I come for you—"

"What do you mean, Victor?"

"He ordered me to slaughter you."

I drop to the ground. I was spared for a long time, allowed to live here all these years for reasons I never fully understood, but now it's over. My time has run out.

"Listen to me." Victor kneels beside me. "Let me drain you to the point of death and leave you to be found here in the morning. There will be no marks on your body, almost no heartbeat. You will appear dead."

"But, Julien—what do I tell him?"

"Nothing. You will be dead, remember? Let him come, bury you, and grieve you. When time has passed, you can return. I will make sure that he is safe."

I run through his plan in my head. I know it's the only way that Ghislain is on a mission to eradicate anyone who is a threat to him. But … "I cannot be buried alive, Victor. … I just—"

"You have nothing to fear. Have I ever let you down?" He kisses me.

I fall shaking into his arms. "What about Julien?"

"I am sure you have made a will, no? Provisions for him?"

"Yes, but—"

"Then let it all play out, Amanda. I will rescue you before anything happens to you, and Julien will be safe, too."

"Why are you doing this for us, Victor?"

He kisses me again. "Because you must be protected. You are more than unique, Amanda. You have power you do not even realize. One day I will return to show you."

He carries me to the rocks and lays me down gently. "I promise you, you will live, my Amanda, and Julien will be safe."

As he cradles me tightly, I close my eyes, feeling only a pinprick. I try to resist at first, but soon I have no choice. I feel myself growing colder, just as I did the night I saved Christian's life on the roof of the Grey Wolf.

It's like I'm slipping away, my spirit rising up through the treetops until I can see the roof of La Maison des Rêves, the kitchen light a beacon in the darkness.

How strange. A figure is running up the gravel drive towards the front door. He looks frazzled and frightened, a state I have never, ever witnessed of my vampire lover Michel. Just before darkness takes me, he glances up into the trees as if he's heard my call.

Epilogue
Julien

Ten years later, 2040—Villepreux

The cab speeds through the sleepy town of Villepreux, exactly as I have remembered it.

I promised myself I would come back one day, even though I could never convince Michel to join me. In fact, he pretty much forbade me to return here.

He opened another Goth club in the West Village, aptly named the Grey Wolf, and was happy amongst mortal women and his vampire friends.

I don't remember much about that night ten years ago, when I got the call to come home after learning of my mother's mysterious death. It all feels like a dream now, even though I am a thirty-year-old man.

A thirty-year-old man who feels like a delinquent for not telling Michel I was coming here. He thinks I am on an assignment in Los Angeles. I did not want to worry him or have to fight him about it.

This is something I have to do. It's time to come home.

What will I find at my childhood home, La Maison des Rêves? Is there someone else living there now?

My hands are sweating as the cab leaves the village, meandering down narrow streets towards the gravel road where my house stood.

I hope to arrive before sunset.

* * *

Amanda

Victor's plan worked perfectly.

Julien did exactly as he was directed and contacted Michel, who promised me a long time ago that he would look after my son, which lifted the heaviest of the burdens from my heart and allowed all the pieces to fall into place. I left him a letter I wrote years ago, confessing Julien's true parentage.

I hope Michel was not too angry with me.

Victor assures me that Christian is alive, but he won't tell me where Ghislain took him after the fire, nor will he tell me how it started.

Michel and Julien fled France for New York. I hoped they would be able to pick up the pieces of their lives.

Victor was true to his word and saved my life again, filling me up with his blood—which, ironically, is Ghislain's blood.

Will I ever return to New York? I suppose someday I might, but for now I need to give Julien and Michel the chance they both have always wanted, though neither of them realizes it.

A chance to be father and son.

Although I have lived a life of deception and secrets, I did it all to save my son and the vampire who fathered him: Michel.

Victor swears he will help me in my search for Christian, though why he would do such a thing, I am not sure. He has, however, always been a most unusual vampire.

And now, so am I.

About the Author

An avid reader since obtaining my first library card, I have always dreamt of publishing novels.
What you hold in your hands is book number three.

Aside from writing, I have spent many years in the business office of a non-profit special-needs school in my home state of New Jersey. A well-deserved shout-out to Montgomery Academy, a place I call home with so many memories and where I feel honored to have served for so many years. Saints one and all. I love you guys more than I can ever express.

An undergraduate degree in anthropology fed my curiosity and awe of Native Americans and non-Western cultures, particularly the head-hunting culture of the Asmat of New Guinea.

Graduate work in museum professions fueled my love of museums and art history. I had the pleasure to briefly intern in the Metropolitan Museum of Art, a place featured in several of my novels and another place I call home.

My obsession with Paris, the Bourbon kings, and the French Revolution spawned my two favorite vampires: Christian Du Mauré and Michel Baptiste, and my childhood obsession with everything metaphysical and paranormal is the thread that weaves through all of my stories.

I thank you for taking the time to read *Eternal Hunger*. It gives me great joy. I speak now for all indie authors when I say that we need your support. If you enjoy our work, spread the word: write a review, tell a friend, share this book with other like-minded readers.

Thank you!

Sincerely,

Denise K. Rago

Where to find me:

www.denisekrago.com
www.facebook.com/dkrago

www.instagram.com/deniseragoauthor
www.twitter.com/DeniseKRago

Guide to Expressions, Places, and Characters in *Eternal Hunger*

A

Ancient Ones An order of Ancient vampires who live belowground in Paris.

Andreas (Captain) Another name for the Ancient vampire Ghislain (ghee-SLAIN).

arrondissement The administrative district of a large French city. Paris has twenty *arrondissements*.

B

Beatrice Maraine Mother of Josette Delacore.

boudoir French for "bedroom."

Bourbons A member of the French royal family that ruled in France from 1589–1792, encompassing Louis XIII through Louis XVI.

bourgeoisie The bourgeois class—the wage-earning class.

Brittany A region in northwest France; a former duchy and province.

brownstone Sandstone used in the construction of a type of building in New York City.

C

cataphile A term for anyone who likes going into the catacombs.

Central Park The largest public park in Manhattan, New York.

Château des Singes A decrepit château somewhere in Normandy, France.

chatelaine The mistress of a castle.

chinois A style of ornamentation in eighteenth-century France characterized by motifs identified as Chinese.

Christian Du Mauré   Eighteenth-century vampire.

Central character to story.

D

déjà vu   The feeling that the situation

currently being experienced has already been experienced in

the past.

Dieu Donné   One of the Ancient Ones.

E

Eléanore Christine Du Mauré   Mother of Christian Du

Mauré.

Étienne   Human servant of Christian Du

Mauré and Michel Baptiste, who is made vampire in the

eighteenth century.

Gabrielle   Vampire of unknown origin

who turns Christian Du Mauré

and Michel Baptiste into

vampires.

Gaétan   An ancient vampire and sworn

enemy of Christian Du Mauré.

Ghislain   A fallen angel who assumes

the guise of a vampire. One of the Ancient Ones.

Greenwich Village   A neighborhood of Manhattan,

home to artists. Commonly known as the Village.

Grey Wolf (club/bar)   Goth club in the East Village

owned by vampires Christian Du Mauré and Michel

Baptiste.

guillotine   An apparatus designed to carry

out executions by beheading. Commonly used during the

French Revolution.

I

Île Saint-Louis One of two natural islands in the Seine River, connected to the rest of Paris by four bridges. Home of Notre-Dame Cathedral.

J

Jardin de Tuileries A public garden located between the Louvre Museum and the Place de la Concorde.

Josette Delacore Eighteenth-century mortal lover to numerous vampires.

Julien Ryan Perretti Son of Amanda Perretti.

K

King Raven King of the Ancient Ones.

L

La Conciergerie Principal prison during the French Revolution. The most famous prisoner was Marie Antoinette.

La Maison des Rêves French for "the house of dreams." The country home of Amanda and Julien Perretti.

Le bal masqué A masked ball.

Le Marais An historic district of Paris. Long the aristocratic district.

Le Pavillon de la Reine Elegant hotel and spa located in the Marais district of Paris.

Louvre Former palace of the French kings. It became a public museum in 1793.

Luc Delacore Husband of Josette Delacore.

M

mademoiselle French title given to a single woman.

Mathieu Son of Josette Delacore and vampire Christian Du Mauré.

Meudon   A small town outside of Paris.

Childhood home to both Christian Du Mauré and Michel

Baptiste.

Michel Baptiste   Childhood friend of Christian

Du Mauré who became vampire in the eighteenth century.

Michel's (club/bar)   The Goth club opened by and

named after Michel Baptiste.

P

Paris   Capital city of France.

Phillipe Du Mauré   Father of Christian Du Mauré.

Pont Neuf   Oldest bridge across the Seine

River in Paris.

Q

Queen Raine   Queen of the Ancient Ones.

Révolution Française   Period of social and political

upheaval in eighteenth-century

France that lasted from 1789 to

1799.

roué   French term for a man who is a

rake, a debaucher.

Rue de Rivoli   One of the most famous streets

in Paris created by Napoleon Bonaparte.

Ryan   Younger brother of Amanda

Perretti.

S

Sabin   Vampire and friend of both

Christian Du Mauré and Michel Baptiste.

Seine   River that runs through Paris.

Solange   Daughter of Josette Delacore

and vampire Michel Baptiste.

Sorbonne   University of Paris.

T

tarot cards   Set of twenty-two cards used

for fortune-telling.

V

Vallée d' Arbres   Ancestral home of vampire

Christian Du Mauré in Meudon,France.

Versailles   Royal château of the French

kings, now a museum.

Victor   One of the Ancient Ones.

Villepreux   Small town outside of Paris.

Location of La Maison des Rêves.

Made in the USA
San Bernardino, CA
16 October 2018